A TALE OF DECEIT

A VERONICA HOWARD VINTAGE MYSTERY

E. J. GANDOLFO

Outskirts Press, Inc.
http://www.outskirtspress.com

ISBN: 978-1-9772-1172-9

PRINTED IN THE UNITED STATES OF AMERICA

This book is dedicated to the memory of my dear parents,
Dr. S. Philip and Elizabeth Gandolfo.

"Oh, what a tangled web we weave . . .
when first we practice to deceive."
Sir Walter Scott

CHAPTER 1

Weather-wise, it was a suitable day for a funeral. The forecast called for cool and overcast conditions, and intermittent rain started to fall just as the graveside service was beginning, lending an appropriate gloom to the proceedings. The plainclothes police in attendance had no trouble identifying the few mourners who were present.

They saw Harold ("Three Fingers Harry") Turner, a legendary safecracker, dressed for the rain in a dark blue anorak with the collar turned up; John ("Rocket") Harmon, a specialist in retrofitting cars so they could make fast getaways, and looking suitably sad as the deceased was his brother-in-law; and Louis ("Louie The Blade") Martin, a skilled pickpocket, who was also handy with knives when the occasion called for it.

Standing together in a tightly knit group, they had come to pay their respects to their former partner in crime, the late jeweler, Earl ("The Eel") Palmer, who always seemed to be able to slither in and out of shady deals and illegal transactions and still come up smelling like a rose. This time, though, his luck had run out, and he was fatally wounded during a police sting operation.

Mortuary personnel and the widow rounded out the mourners. Today, Justine Harmon Palmer was feeling neither sad nor bereft because her late husband had always been a disappointment to her. In fact, it was a major source of comfort to know that she no longer had to explain to friends and family why she had married Earl in the first place. He had met his end while taking part in a highly publicized robbery, and the newspapers had been carrying the story for days now. She was embarrassed to show her face in Bromfield, and the only option left to her was to play the innocent wife to the hilt. Justine was sure most people would just assume that she had played an active role in Earl's illegal activities when that was not the case. Public opinion was important to her, and now that Earl was dead, she would have to work very hard to reinforce her standing as the deceived and unsuspecting widow of a thief.

Then, there was her brother, John. It was bad enough that he had served jail time for his part in one of Earl's schemes to get rich quickly by relieving people of their jewelry, but why did he have to show up with his dubious friends today, of all days? She glanced over her shoulder. Weren't the two men standing over by the monument erected to honor Bromfield's fallen soldiers the police? She wondered, not for the first time, when it was all going to end.

Across town, Veronica Howard, known to her friends as "Ronnie," was turning on the lights in her antique store, "Veronica's Vintage," preparing to open for the day. It had always been her dream to start her own vintage clothing and antique business, and after spending many years working as an advertising agency copywriter, the opportunity presented itself to her one day in the form of a pink slip, laying her off from her job. Her agency had been bought out, and it became clear the new owners had no plans to retain her, no matter how popular she was with her coworkers or how valuable her services were to her clients.

She realized that this was the impetus she needed to take steps to start her own business finally. She had always talked herself out of moving forward: the timing wasn't quite right yet, the economy wasn't as strong as it should be, the comfort of a secure paycheck was not to be despised, the friends she had made over the years at work were like a family, etc. The time for excuses had now passed. But once she had found the perfect location for her store in Bromfield, a town twelve miles north of Boston on the ocean, signed the lease, and put up the sign over the door, the years of dreams were finally becoming a reality.

Veronica was an attractive woman in her middle years blessed with shiny black hair worn in a fashionable bob cut, cat-green eyes, a creamy complexion, and long, shapely legs. Not quite totally giving in to myopia but more of a fashion statement, she frequently wore her trademark harlequin eyeglasses on the end of her nose. Her nails were usually painted crimson as were her lips, and if she had been born during the Roaring Twenties, she would have been described as a very stylish flapper.

Veronica's clothing choices usually turned heads, and she long ago gave up the notion that blending in with everyone else's idea of fashion was not going to work for her. Her unique individuality and upbeat personality made her stand out in a crowd, and it didn't hurt either that she was an intelligent woman.

If she had any negative attributes, one would have to say that she became bored easily, and was, at times, overly inquisitive. Her mind was quick, and she always had an insatiable curiosity about people. She possessed the uncanny ability to be able to cut through the rhetoric and identify people who were not quite what they appeared to be. Sometimes, though, that ability let her down, and because she was a woman, she let her feelings influence her opinions.

She was pleased with the way her life was going now that she had opened her shop, but the specter of boredom was always lying just beneath the surface. It was as if her contentment was built on quicksand rather than solid ground.

Veronica was aware that when she was born, she had a caul, a piece of the amniotic sac, over her face, or a "veil," as it was known in folklore. The old wives' tale told to her mother was that her baby would grow up to have special powers or the "second sight." They said she would always have the ability to see into the future because of this unusual birth phenomenon and enjoy a life of good luck. Some attributed the legend of being born with a caul to St. Veronica, who wiped the face of Christ with her veil; hence, "Veronica's Veil," and the inspiration for her mother to name her child after the saint.

Veronica's boyfriend, Harry, always told her that she was just plain nosy and "second sight" had nothing to do with it. As far as perpetual good luck went, Veronica knew she shouldn't hold her breath waiting for it to appear any-time soon. She did realize, however, that sometimes she experienced a tingling sensation down her spine, and that, somehow, seemed to predict that something was going to happen to her soon that was not going to be an everyday occurrence. She couldn't really act on this sensation until circumstances revealed themselves. If that was a "second sight," then Veronica had to admit that, yes, she did, indeed, possess it.

———————◦«◦»◦———————

Veronica's Vintage was located on Posy Place, a quaint street the real estate developers endeavored to make more picturesque by adding cobblestone sidewalks and old-fash-ioned street lamps. In the summertime, hanging baskets of fuchsia and wrought iron containers of petunias and ge-raniums above the storefronts added a seasonal touch. In the winter, boughs of evergreen branches and holly berries and wreaths with bright red bows made the street look fes-tive and inviting. Her immediate neighbors included a cozy flower shop and a trendy hair salon, and the daily delicious aromas of freshly baked bread wafting from the bakery down the street ensured that the area was a popular destination for foot traffic. Business had been good almost since the day she opened, and Veronica found it necessary to hire a full-time helper, Susan, who enjoyed working in a vintage shop that sold "cool" things.

Joe Banks, the well liked and longtime local beat cop, had the habit of taking his morning coffee break at Veronica's store, and today he brought with him freshly baked croissants. He liked to share the local gossip, and today was no exception.

"Morning, Joe," said Veronica, reaching into the bag. "I'm guessing that you don't mind a chance to get out of the rain."

"You eat more of these than I do," he laughed, "so how come I have the weight problem, and you don't?"

"I'd say it was the luck of the draw, and let's not forget the gene pool."

The bell tinkled over the door announcing the first customer of the day. A short, plump woman with gray hair swept up in a ponytail and a determined air bustled in the door. She looked around the store and walked over to a rack of clothing while explaining she was an English teacher at Bromfield High School and advisor to the dramatic society. She asked if Veronica had any period clothing they could rent for their upcoming play which takes place in the 1920s.

Veronica thought a moment and said the items on

display were not available to rent. However, she did have some clothing she would be glad to donate if they wouldn't mind some minor stains. The woman was overjoyed and said she would return the next day to look them over.

"That's kind of you, if I do say so," said Joe, munching on his pastry.

"I'm always glad to help, but I think I will have to go to the weekly flea market on Sunday to see if I can find some additional items for them. The weather is supposed to be great, and I'll talk Harry into coming with me."

Veronica's boyfriend, Harry Hunt, the son of a wealthy Boston Brahmin family, was not known to hold a steady job. But she had recently discovered to her great surprise that Harry had another life of which she was entirely unaware. Like Veronica, Harry lived in Boston. He was devoted to her, and their comfortable relationship had been happy for the three years that they had known each other. Neither had the inclination to marry, and they found that the situation suited them both. In order to protect his undercover law enforcement status, Harry still maintained the outward signs of a rich dilettante who had the enviable ability to possess great wealth without seeming to have to work for a living.

There was a sign in the window of Veronica's Vintage that announced: "Always Buying Antique & Vintage Items." She knew from experience that some items people had thought of as old because their grandmother owned them were not necessarily old at all. A large part of the enjoyment of having a store was that she was able to explain to her customers where and when the merchandise that she sold was made and the history behind each piece. People were always eager to hear stories about their ancestors; how they lived, the objects they possessed, and what they valued.

By popular demand, Veronica started to schedule monthly lectures in the evenings at the store. Sometimes, people brought items to be appraised and were often surprised to hear the current market worth. Some were disappointed to learn that what they had always thought was a cherished family heirloom wasn't really old at all. And, as was often the case, the reality that an item always thought to be worth a fortune turned out to be of no particular monetary value at all.

The monthly lecture for June was to be held that evening, and Veronica busied herself, putting out the coffee and tea urns while Susan set up chairs in the center of the shop. Tonight, the topic was jewelry made during the Victorian period, always a popular subject. Twenty-five people attended, and after the lecture, several brought their family pieces to her to appraise.

She was about to close for the evening when a drab-looking young woman with a detached air approached and asked if she would examine a piece of jewelry that she said was probably worthless. She followed Veronica over to her desk where the light was better, then reached into a battered leather shoulder bag and pulled out a torn length of newspaper. Veronica's breath left her when a glittering necklace slipped out. She reached for her jeweler's loupe and carefully examined the piece, a wonderful example of an Art Deco pendant with a matching chain made of diamonds and platinum.

Looking up at the woman in wonder, Veronica asked how she had come to own such a beautiful object. She shrugged her shoulders and said she found it in one of the pockets of some old clothing she inherited.

"What's it worth?" she asked. Veronica told her it was valuable and inquired if she had any other items like it.

"Maybe," the woman said coyly, "but I wanna sell the clothes first."

"I would be interested in looking at your old clothing and anything else you might have to sell."

The woman, who identified herself only as Mary, said she would be setting up at the Bromfield weekly outdoor flea market on Sunday.

"Well, what will ya give me for this?" she asked, wiping her nose on her sleeve.

Suddenly, it occurred to Veronica that the necklace could be stolen, and her story didn't really add up. Illegal drugs were a problem in Bromfield, as in any upscale town these days, but her natural curiosity prompted her to ask Mary to promise to hold on to the necklace for her at least until Sunday's flea market, two days away. After she left the store, Veronica rushed over to the phone and called Harry. He listened quietly as she recounted her experience, then asked her what she thought the necklace's appraisal would be.

"Oh, Harry, it has to be worth at least $3,000. The metal is platinum, and the diamonds are genuinely old, mine-cut stones of good size and excellent quality; true period Art Deco and absolutely gorgeous."

"It seems rather far-fetched that she found it in the pocket of some old clothes," said Harry. "More than likely, it was found in someone's jewelry box in a house that was burgled."

"I told her I would meet her at the Bromfield Flea Market on Sunday at dawn to look at other things she has for sale. Will you come with me?"

"Of course, but don't be surprised if she isn't there. It sounds as if she needs the money right away, and you told her the necklace is valuable."

"I just have to follow through now that my curiosity is aroused."

"Ah, the old 'Veronica curiosity' comes through again," he sighed. "It's a good thing I'm an early riser."

She didn't tell Harry that she was experiencing a tingling sensation down her spine. No need to put herself in the position of being teased again by her skeptical boyfriend.

CHAPTER 2

The Bromfield Flea Market, a summer and early fall institution for over thirty years, is held weekly in a rural farm field on Sunday mornings during the season with room for about two hundred sellers. The dealers drive their trucks and overloaded cars in at first light and start selling to those eager to buy the fresh pickings from estate sales and house cleanouts. This morning the weather was cool and the grass dewy from the rain of the night before. The delicious aroma of freshly brewing coffee and frying bacon from the canteen wagon invigorated the early bird buyers who darted between the aisles looking for a rare find.

When Veronica and Harry drove in to the parking lot, the sun was just coming up. The forecast was for a slightly cool and clear morning, good enough to entice even the most reluctant buyers to get up at dawn. Those dealers who had trucks and vans didn't even have time to unload their merchandise. Customers eager to grab the odd pieces of furniture, lamps, vintage store signs, and other curiosities just jumped aboard and helped themselves. China and glass were hastily laid out on folding tables, and cardboard boxes were thrown on the ground for those who preferred to forage for a bargain.

They were caught up in the excitement, and Veronica was determined to locate the booth of the woman who identified herself only as Mary. Harry followed Veronica up and down the aisles for about half an hour when they finally spotted a dented and rusty car in a far corner of the field with a blanket in front of it piled high with old clothing. Mary was sitting on the driver's side, smoking a cigarette, and got out of the car when she saw Veronica approach.

"Who's this?" she asked abruptly, pointing at Harry.

"This is my friend, Harry, and he likes flea markets as much as I do," she explained, eyeing the mound of clothes. They had agreed beforehand not to make too much of the necklace, and Veronica started to pick through the clothing.

Setting aside some items, she casually asked the girl if she had anything else to sell. Mary didn't answer right away and seemed to be looking up the aisle searching for someone.

"May I get you a cup of coffee, Mary?" asked Harry. "You must be cold."

"No, thanks," she sniffed. "I'm waiting for my boyfriend to come back with one." A minute later, a skinny, young man with a sallow, pockmarked complexion arrived carrying a cardboard box containing two cups of coffee and four donuts. She introduced him as Eddie, and he immediately asked her if Veronica was the one she showed the necklace to.

"Yes, I am, and I'm still interested in it and any other

pieces you have."

"Are you gonna buy these clothes now?" asked Eddie, pointing to the small pile on the ground.

"Sure, but I want to see what else you have," she said, getting into the spirit of things.

Mary nodded to Eddie, and he walked silently to the trunk and took out a small, velvet jewelry box, motioning with his head for them to come over. Veronica didn't dare take out her jeweler's loupe, but she recognized instantly the exceptional quality of the pieces winking at her in the early-morning light. The two rings, a pair of earrings, and a pin were the same high quality as the necklace Mary had shown her at the store. Harry stood silently with his hands in his pockets looking bored, but he knew full well he was looking at exceptional, top-of-the-line period jewelry.

"What do you want for the whole box?" asked Veronica, trying to look nonchalant.

Eddie thought for a minute, then asked if she wanted to buy the necklace as well.

"It depends on how much you want for them."

"Cash?" he asked, and Veronica nodded yes.

"Okay, gimme five hundred for all of it."

She looked at Harry who quickly peeled off five one hundred-dollar bills from a roll of cash that he deliberately flaunted. Eddie's eyes lit up when he saw the money and, without a word, shoved the box at her and quickly pocketed the bills. Veronica asked once again if there was anything else for sale.

"Mary's got more clothes in the backseat," he said and opened the car door. The quality of the items she pulled out was exquisite. There were beaded flapper dresses, embroidered silk gowns, some with matching shoes, and a wonderful silk velvet coat and scarf in the Deco Chinese style. She carefully placed these items alongside her original pile and asked for a price for the entire lot.

While they were negotiating, Harry noticed out of the corner of his eye two seedy-looking men standing off to the side listening attentively to the conversation. Eddie also noticed them and snarled at Mary to hurry up and finish so they could leave. A price was finally arrived at and this time Veronica opened her wallet and paid, asking again if she had seen everything they had brought to sell. Mary glanced at Eddie and said she would come to the store during the week with other items for sale. They packed the clothing in paper bags and walked back to the parking lot.

"I want to put these things in my locked trunk," said Harry and he piled everything into the Porsche. They were about to drive away when it suddenly occurred to Veronica that she should have given Mary her phone number and business card.

"Do you mind if we go back to see them again?" she asked. Harry put the car in gear and was about to back out when they suddenly heard a piercing scream and several voices shouting. They both glanced at each other then jumped out of the car to see people running in the direction of Mary and Eddie's booth. They quickly followed the crowd and arrived in time to notice a Bromfield Police squad car with flashing blue lights speeding up the main road. They ran to the booth and saw Mary kneeling on the ground beside a prone Eddie, shaking his body and repeatedly crying out his name. Eddie had a knife protruding from his stomach and wasn't moving. The police arrived and pushed the onlookers back. Mary was crying hysterically while trying to explain that two men rushed them while they were packing to leave. They exchanged angry words, and one of them took out a knife and stabbed him. Harry approached one of the officers and identified themselves as customers who had just left the booth minutes before and gave the police a description of the two men.

They were asked to come to the police station and give their statements and were met with a nod from the desk sergeant and a polite handshake from Lieutenant Phil Balducci, who remembered them from the recent art heist and murder affair. A pleasant-looking, slightly overweight man with a full head of iron-gray hair and bushy dark eyebrows, his hearty manner didn't quite mask his shrewd, dark brown eyes that registered everything.

"Well, well, we meet again," said the lieutenant. "Murder seems to follow you two around like a shadow." He invited them to sit down and tell him what they saw, watching them closely with a mixture of amusement and interest, while quietly sitting with his arms folded across his chest.

"Why do I get the feeling I'm not hearing the whole story?" he asked finally, reaching for a licorice stick from the canister on his desk and chewing on it thoughtful-ly. "Strawberry, my favorite," he murmured, by way of explanation.

"Lieutenant," Veronica asked, "why are you chewing licorice?"

"I'm trying to give up smoking, and my wife suggested I try this."

"Is it working?" she asked.

"Not really, but it gives me something to do with my hands. I repeat, what are you leaving out, and why would you show up at dawn on a Sunday morning just to buy some old clothes?"

"It's my business, Lieutenant, you know, to buy and sell vintage clothing." She handed him her business card. "The woman came to my shop and invited me to the flea market to see what she had to sell. While I was paying her for the items, we noticed the two men hanging around the booth. It's as simple as that."

He sighed and pressed the intercom button on the phone. "We'll show you some mug shots and the sketch art-ist will draw what you remember." He reached into his desk drawer. "Here's my card, in case you think of anything else I should know about. You know the drill, Mr. Hunt, as well as I do. I wouldn't like to think an undercover Special Agent for the FBI is holding out on me."

Harry smiled. "Not a chance, Lieutenant; not a chance."

Back in the car, Veronica asked Harry why he didn't men-tion the jewelry. "I don't want the police to know about it just yet. It's possible the jewelry is part of a major robbery that we are currently investigating, and until I can check our records, I think it's wise to keep quiet about it for now."

She reached over and took out the jewelry case from the glove compartment. "What beautiful pieces," she sighed. "I know I would be devastated if I lost all of this to a robber, but something tells me Mary has more, much more, somewhere. I wish we knew how to get in touch with her. She looked so pathetic kneeling there on the ground. At least, I can keep the clothing I bought from her."

"Veronica, you can't keep the clothing or the jewelry," Harry said firmly. "They've probably all been stolen, no matter how much you don't want to admit it, and it all has to be turned over to the police as evidence, eventually."

She looked over at him and nodded. "I know, I know, but I can dream, can't I?"

CHAPTER 3

The events of the morning gave them an appetite, and they decided to have lunch at their favorite North Shore Thai Restaurant. The smiling owner led them to a quiet corner table. The sound of the nearby fountain quietly splashing water over a rock formation lulled them into peaceful contemplation. They ordered Shumai dumplings, yellow curry, and sticky rice. The spicy meal was delicious, and they finished with coconut ice cream and hot tea.

They decided Harry would lock the jewelry box in his home safe and take photos of all the items and bring them to the office in the morning to check the records. After eating, they drove back to the shop and unloaded the clothing from the car. The store was closed on Sunday, and she was able to lay them out on a table to inspect for damage without attending to customers. Veronica marveled at the quality and workmanship and told Harry that a wealthy lady must have owned them as they were most likely all custom-made. In fact, she thought, I can just picture Aunt Gillian wearing these garments, as she had owned similar styles.

While Harry read the newspaper, she busied herself by hanging each item on a rack. When she finally got to the silk velvet Chinese coat, she noticed a small lump in the hem. She tried to smooth it out with her fingers and was surprised to discover it wasn't a wrinkle at all but something hard under the fabric. She reached for a small pair of scissors and carefully snipped a few stitches. To her great surprise, a piece of jewelry fell out.

"Oh my God," she cried.

Harry threw down the paper he was reading and rushed over. In her hand was an exquisite, period diamond and platinum cocktail ring. "It was sewn into the hem, Harry," she said in wonder. "Can you imagine?"

She took her jeweler's loupe from the desk drawer and carefully inspected the ring. "It has to be at least 3 carats," she whispered in reverence. The stone twinkled back at her as she turned it in the light.

"More evidence we have to keep to ourselves for the moment," he said, while she slipped the beautiful ring on and quietly admired it.

After a while he gently tried to pry it from her finger and she looked into his eyes. The thought was going through her mind that she would give anything to own an antique ring exactly like this one and Harry was the only man she knew who could afford to buy such an expensive jewel.

"Come on, Veronica," he urged, "give it to me, and I'll put it with the rest of the stash."

Reluctantly, she let him take it off while thinking she would absolutely die if someone stole such a treasure from her.

"The ring must have been sewn into the garment hem for safekeeping," Harry observed. "Not the usual place to hide something so valuable, but it sure beats an ice cube tray in the refrigerator for novelty."

She couldn't help but wonder if there were more treasures like this in the rest of the clothing Mary had for sale. I really wish I could get in touch with her, she thought.

———◦《◦》◦———

She didn't have long to wait. The next day around noon, the bell over the door heralded the arrival of a customer, and she looked up from her desk to see Mary walk in the door. She rushed over to the girl and ushered her to a chair. Mary's eyes were red from weeping, and her slumped shoulders made her look like a dejected rag doll. Veronica made her a cup of sweet coffee and asked her how she was feeling.

"The cops had me answering questions for hours. I never thought Eddie and me would end up like this."

Veronica sat quietly and let her talk. It seemed Eddie was her boyfriend and drug supplier. They met at a rehab group and had been living together for a couple of years. He had a record of petty theft and had heard of the possibility of a big score from the two men Veronica and Harry had seen at the flea market. They broke into the residence of a wealthy old lady who lived alone in a mansion by the ocean and took what they could carry before the cook discovered them and called the police. Mary fell in love with the clothing, and the plan was for the gang to return in a few days and take more.

They needed money for food and that's why Mary came to Veronica's Vintage the night of the jewelry lecture. She suspected the jewelry might be more than costume, but they were broke and desperate. The two men followed them to the flea market and saw Harry pay with a large roll of bills. A fight ensued and Eddie refused to give them any of the money that they claimed was their share from the burglary. Mary hadn't noticed which one had the knife.

The police were aware that Eddie had a record but she had never been arrested before. Mary always had jobs as a waitress, working in various places because they moved around a lot. She needed rent money today and asked Veronica if she would buy what was left in their apartment. Veronica felt bad for the girl and agreed to go with her to look at what she had.

"It's not all stolen, ya know, but I guess I won't need any of it now." She sniffed and started to cry again.

They stopped at the bakery and Veronica bought her a sandwich to eat there and another to take out. She wondered what had happened to the five hundred dollars Harry paid Eddie at the flea market but didn't ask. They drove to a seedy section of town and parked in front of a run-down apartment building. Smells of cooked cabbage and grease permeated the hallway, and the sounds of a wailing baby followed them as they walked up the four flights to her one-bedroom apartment.

An unmade bed and plates stacked high in the sink greeted them along with several large cardboard cartons stacked and overflowing with clothes. Everywhere Veronica looked clothing was thrown in heaps on the floor, on the bed, and stuffed in closets.

"We was going to move again if we couldn't come up with the rent," said Mary, following Veronica's eyes as she looked around the room.

"My friend Tiffani says I can crash with her until I get a job."

Veronica was only interested in the vintage items and found a carton containing more beautiful pieces.

"There's some more here and over there too," said Mary, pointing to another box. It contained shoes and several Deco mesh bags and compacts.

This is like a treasure hunt, she thought, happily adding more items to a pile. Veronica knew she couldn't keep them but enjoyed owning them if only for a little while.

"I will pay you for these, Mary, but as they are stolen, I will have to turn them over to the police as evidence. Is there any more jewelry?"

Mary hesitated a moment, then walked over to the closet, rummaged around on the floor, and took out a shoe box and a small paper bag. She handed the bag to Veronica. It contained a cheap plastic bracelet.

"Come on, Mary, what's in the box?" she said, losing

patience. "I'm not a big fan of being deceived."

The girl shoved it at her, then sat on the edge of the bed, sulking.

Veronica took off the cover to reveal the precious contents of an elaborate Edwardian lady's diamond wristwatch, a diamond stickpin in the shape of a fox's head, and a pair of white gold and diamond cuff links. She glanced over at Mary who could see the look of astonishment on Veronica's face.

"Eddie told me he just grabbed what was on the old lady's bureau," she explained.

"You could get serious jail time for this, Mary, as an accessory to grand theft." Mary's eyes widened in horror at this news.

"I don't need any of it. Just, just give it back," she stuttered and started to cry again. "I don't want no trouble with the cops. Honest."

Veronica didn't have the heart to see Mary go to prison. She gave her fifty dollars for the clothes, told her to put it toward the rent, and look for another job in the morning.

CHAPTER 4

She took everything back to the store and called Harry. He answered the phone on the first ring. "I've been trying to reach you; I have news," he said.

"So have I, but you go first."

"I had another little chat with Lieutenant Phil Balducci. The police think they have identified the two suspects, thanks to our description and the drawings. "This ain't my first rodeo"; he laughed, "and there is an all-points bulletin search out for them." Just at that moment, Harry's other phone rang. It was the Bromfield Police Department. "I'll call you right back," he said.

Veronica sat and waited, wondering if she had done the right thing by buying the rest of the items from Mary. She glanced over at the boxes and realized with a sinking heart that the beautiful clothing she had coveted would have to be returned to their rightful owner. If the shoe were on the other foot, she would have been delighted to get them back and knew the lady who owned them would feel the same way.

Harry called back. "They've caught the two men, and we have been summoned to a lineup at the police station.

They will require us to make a formal identification tomorrow morning. Now, what's your news?"

She recounted her afternoon with Mary and described the merchandise she recovered. Harry didn't answer right away.

"Hello, are you there?"

"I'm thinking," he said. "You do know, Veronica, that you still have to turn over the clothing and jewelry to the police, don't you?"

"If that is a rhetorical question, I know when you use that tone of voice that you mean business."

He sighed heavily. "Look, I know you love all those things, and I wish you could keep them too, but it's just not possible."

"Okay, don't rub it in, but I would like to return them myself to the rightful owner and see her delighted expression when she gets them back."

Harry picked her up the next morning and they went to the police station where Lieutenant Balducci, who was chewing on a licorice stick, met them.

"What flavor is it this time?" she asked.

"Cherry," he said. "Not my all-time favorite."

They walked to the interrogation room and stood behind the one-way mirror. There were eight men lined up facing them. "Take your time," said Balducci, and he turned to an officer who was holding a clipboard. "Ready when you are, Anderson."

"Turn left," barked Officer Anderson into the microphone.

Harry squinted at the mirror, and Veronica put on her harlequin eyeglasses. "It's tough getting old," quipped the lieutenant.

"Turn right."

"Numbers four and seven," said Veronica, nodding in the affirmative.

"Yes, I agree," said Harry.

Balducci pointed at them with the licorice stick. "Sure about that?"

"Yes," they said in unison.

"Got that, Anderson?"

"Yes, sir. They've ID'd both suspects."

They all walked back to the squad room and sat down. "You've had the honor of identifying two of Bromfield's more colorful occupants of our Most Wanted List: one Harold Turner, also known as 'Three Fingers Harry' and Louis Martin, or 'Louie the Blade'. They've been on our radar for some time now. It will be a pleasure putting these 'two upstanding citizens' away. Their greed has finally gotten the better of them, and I want to thank you for helping us with this."

Veronica asked if she could have the name of the woman who was robbed, and the lieutenant could think of no reason why she shouldn't have it. He wrote a name on the notepad and handed the piece of paper to her.

Mrs. Matilda Van Brockhurst lived on Water Crest Drive, off a winding shore road facing the Atlantic Ocean. Her imposing mansion, "Sea Spray," was pink stucco, built in the Italianate style, and hidden from the road behind a high wall fortified with an elaborate black wrought iron fence. Built in the Newport "cottage" style of vast summer homes owned by the nation's wealthiest citizens before taxes and the stock market crash, "Sea Spray" was originally occupied for only one or two months a year and required a large staff to run. Now it was inhabited year-round by Mrs. Van Brockhurst, a grand dame in her early nineties. She had been a widow for about twenty years, and her late husband was the wealthy son of a well-known steel and railroad family. She was childless and had always devoted her life to charity work.

Veronica called to make an appointment and explained who she was. The butler, Fiske, was the quintessential servant who ruled the remaining staff with an iron hand. He answered the door dressed in a uniform of striped pants, vest and jacket and looked cadaverous with his slight build and bald head. "Madam is expecting you, miss. Please, come in," he intoned, stiff and unsmiling.

She was ushered into a beautifully appointed morning room decorated in a formal French style. The day was bright and clear and the sun streamed in through the sixteen-foot-high windows that took up most of one wall that faced the ocean. Draperies of burgundy and yellow-striped silk grazed the huge oriental carpet, the designs of which mirrored the same shades. The cream walls were hung with Impressionist paintings and a gilt wood French lady's desk held a Tiffany lead glass lamp with a dragonfly motif. Veronica stood waiting and heard the steady *tick-tock* of the grandfather clock, breaking the silence of the rest of the house.

After a few minutes the sound of wheels on the carpet heralded the arrival of the lady of the house. Veronica turned to see a nurse dressed in a white cap and uniform, pushing a wheelchair inhabited by an elderly lady wearing a pale-blue silk dressing gown. Her pure-white hair was beautifully arranged in short waves around her fully made up face. She smiled sweetly and extended her hand.

"I'm so very glad to meet you, Miss Howard," she said in a soft voice. "I understand I owe you a great deal of thanks for retrieving the items that were stolen from me.

"Please, sit down, and may I offer you some refreshment? Alice, please bring us tea," she said to the hovering maid. "Fiske has been on the telephone to the police department and I believe the two thieves have been apprehended."

"Yes, they have, but now the case has been upgraded to murder," explained Veronica, filling in the details.

"How shocking this whole business is. We still can't fathom why this house was targeted. I've lived here for over fifty years, and there has never been anything like this before. My neighbors still can't believe it."

"I know the police are holding your jewelry and clothing as evidence. My purpose in coming here today is strictly personal. I wanted to meet the woman who owns such beautiful things."

The old lady smiled. "How delightful, my dear. Please tell me a little something about yourself."

As they sipped tea, she found it easy to talk to this charming woman. There was an aura about her of the genteel, but something told her that perhaps she was not born to this life. In fact, Mrs. Van Brockhurst reminded Veronica very much of Aunt Gillian.

"I have so little company, you see," she explained, and she encouraged Veronica to talk to her about her life. Veronica could see the old lady was lonely, so she told her of her former life as a typist and copywriter, then her desire to open her own business, a shop that offered beautiful vintage clothing and antique objects for sale. She described Veronica's Vintage in detail and the merchandise the store contained, even down to the portrait of her beloved aunt. She recounted stories about her customers and funny anecdotes about some of the house calls and incidents she encountered while trying to buy stock for her store.

Presently, she glanced over and noticed her companion sitting quietly with hands folded on her lap, eyes closed, a little smile on her face, the muted but constant *tick-tock* of the clock the only sound to be heard in the house. Suddenly, Mrs. Van Brockhurst's eyes opened, and she asked her guest why she had stopped speaking. Realizing she was listening and not napping, Veronica continued. She spoke of her lonely childhood and of being adopted by her aunt who was her role model and the positive effect she had on her life. Her voice became animated while describing the fun they had together going through old trunks in Gillian's attic.

"Would you mind moving me over to the window?" she asked at one point. Veronica got up and pushed the wheelchair to the huge picture window overlooking the ocean. As far as the eye could see, the cloudless blue sky met the gray horizon in a steady, unending line, giving an ethereal look to the ocean. They gazed out quietly through the window together, each lost in her own reverie, the hypnotic pull of the vista both calming and soothing.

Eventually the nurse reappeared and reminded her patient it was time for her medication and a nap.

"I'm so sorry if I have tired you," said Veronica. "I didn't realize how much time I've taken to tell you my stories."

"Don't apologize, my dear. I can't remember when I've enjoyed myself as much. Promise me you will return soon for another visit. Just call Fiske and he will arrange it."

Veronica thanked her hostess and Fiske led her to the door. "I hope I haven't overstayed my welcome with Mrs. Van Brockhurst."

"She doesn't have too many visitors these days, miss," he said in a stiff and haughty voice.

I don't like that man, she thought, and walked down the cobblestone circular driveway to her car, past the massive fountain depicting three bronze dolphins spouting cascades of water.

CHAPTER 5

Back at the store Veronica and Susan busied themselves with changing the window displays. It was important to keep people interested in the merchandise, and rotating the stock was a must twice a week. Today Veronica chose more vintage items than antique. The bright orange and lime-green geometric print mod dress with white patent leather go-go boots was a 1960s' statement. On either side of the dress manikin they arranged platform-soled shoes and plastic handbags in bright citrus colors. The growing clientele of thirty-somethings was attracted to the era their mothers remembered with fondness and nostalgia. Susan's mother, Kathy, one of the store's best customers, walked by on her way to the hairdresser and gave them an enthusiastic thumbs-up approval for the display.

Later in the morning, someone tapped on the window and Veronica looked up to see her friend, Diane Andrews, smiling and holding up two coffees. She waved her in the door and they embraced. Diane was the ex-wife of the murdered Carl who was part of a ring of art thieves that Veronica and Harry helped to break up. Diane had moved on with her life and found a good job at the library and a new man who adored her.

They sipped their coffees and caught up. Veronica told her about Mrs. Van Brockhurst and the robbery.

"How you could bear to part with those beautiful clothes and jewelry is a mystery to me," said Diane. "I'm sure the lady was overjoyed to know she would finally be getting them back."

"I really like her, Diane, but her butler is another story. Something tells me he is not to be trusted."

The bell over the door heralded the arrival of her favorite beat cop, Joe Banks.

"Just in time for donuts to go with your coffees, ladies," he said, placing a box on the counter. He joined in the gossip, and when Lt. Phil Balducci's name came up, Joe went quiet for a minute.

"Best damn cop I ever met," he said with feeling. "Instinct's like a real Hercule Poirot and just as mysterious."

"Only, instead of a mustache, he has a licorice stick," giggled Veronica.

—————— ((•)) ——————

Veronica had decided to go back to the flea market again on the following Sunday and asked Harry to accompany her but he had a family obligation to attend to and couldn't put it off. She asked Diane to go instead and she happily agreed. They pulled in to the parking lot at 7:00 a.m. and, as usual, it was full of the cars of customers who had been shopping since dawn. They dressed in rubber boots as it had rained the night before, and warm sweaters and tote bags, the uniform for the hardy types who shopped here regularly. As the sun came up, sweaters were discarded and flashlights turned off, and the buying began in earnest.

Row after row of tables offered diverse items for sale of every size and description. Diane found a small drop leaf mahogany table in the first aisle that she deemed perfect for her apartment. She bargained and got a better price and told the dealer she would pick it up later. Veronica was looking for vintage items and was able to buy an undamaged carved Bakelite purse and a compact from the 1950s with a confetti glitter top. Both pieces would give her a nice profit at the store.

They stopped for a cold drink around midmorning and a rest at a picnic table. It was starting to get hot and crowded. The flea market was a popular venue for an inexpensive family outing with lots of young mothers pushing baby carriages and men walking their dogs. They agreed to give the place another half hour and then head home. Veronica was hoping to buy vintage clothing and was disappointed at the lack of potential stock for the store. Suddenly, she spotted a pile of clothes on a blanket on the table opposite where they were resting. She darted across the aisle and pulled out two 1920s' jackets, both in the Chinese style, almost exactly like the one she bought from Mary and owned by Mrs. Van Brockhurst.

"How much for these jackets?" she asked, as the dealer was unloading more items from the trunk of his car. He scratched his beard for a moment and said he would sell them both for fifty dollars. She knew she should bargain, but the quality was such that she pulled out her wallet and paid the asking price immediately.

"Do you have any others?" she asked hopefully. He said he didn't and had only just bought the two pieces a few minutes before from another dealer on the field. As she was folding them to put into her tote bag, Veronica noticed the monogram on an inside hem—"MVB." She stopped in her tracks, and it suddenly dawned on her what she was holding and who owned it.

"If you show me the person you bought these from, I'll give you a twenty dollar-finder's fee right now," she said. The man almost jumped over the table and stepped in front of her to search the field. "There she is, over there. The woman with the blond hair," he said, pointing down the aisle. "Come on; I'll walk you over."

She followed him to a table that was stacked high with various items, some more clothing, but mostly quality pieces of cut glass and good china. The dealer was talking to a man who was trying to negotiate a better price for a beautiful mid-century Italian glass vase, so Veronica hastily began to go through the pile and found three treasures immediately. One was an exquisite Edwardian tea gown in oyster-grey silk chiffon with black bugle bead trim. The label read "Paul Poiret, Paris," and she trembled when she read it. She knew he was a world-famous couturier of his time, on a par with Coco Chanel, and designed only for the very wealthy. The other two items also had Paris labels.

Diane spotted Veronica, waved, and was about to call out her name when she motioned to her to keep silent. They waited patiently until the vase transaction was completed. The woman turned around, stared at Veronica for a few seconds, and asked if she could help.

It immediately occurred to Veronica that this dealer looked familiar, but she couldn't remember where she had seen her before. "Yes, I'm interested in these three items. What is your best price?"

"Oh, I'm sorry. These are already sold," said the dealer. "I'm just waiting for the customer to pick them up."

Veronica was not about to give in. "But they were out on the table for sale and at the bottom of this pile."

The woman smiled, shrugged her shoulders, but didn't answer.

Veronica was persistent. "I like them enough to make you an offer. Would three hundred dollars be fair?"

The beady, pale-blue eyes blinked once and the nose quivered. In that split second Veronica was sure she could place the face.

"Well, how can I say no to an offer like that," she replied and reached for wrapping paper and a bag. Veronica paid, thanked her, and swiftly walked away.

Diane hurried after her to catch up. "What's going on?" she panted.

"Let's pick up your table, and I'll tell you all about it."

They drove out of the flea market and down the street to a home-made ice cream stand. "My treat," said Veronica, and they took their cones to a table under a maple tree.

"Well, are you going to tell me where you know that blond from and what the big secret is?" nagged Diane.

Veronica licked her cone and smiled a cat's smile. "That blond isn't really blond. In fact, 'she' is really a 'he' with no hair at all!"

"What are you talking about, Ronnie? You've lost me completely."

"The person who just sold me these three gorgeous pieces of vintage clothing is Mrs. Van Brockhurst's butler, Fiske, in a blond wig. And, furthermore, these are *her* clothes, part of the stolen property that Harry and I recovered at this very flea market last week."

Diane finally found her voice. "But how do you know this?"

Veronica showed her the coat she purchased from the first dealer and the MVB monogram on the inside seam. She explained that the dealer had just purchased it from Fiske, who had more of her items in his booth. She had to buy them back as proof that he had something to do with Mrs. Van Brockhurst's theft of her family heirlooms and as further evidence in the murder investigation of Mary's boyfriend.

"But why would he disguise himself as a woman and set up at the local flea market?"

"I'm sure he never expected to see someone shopping

here who could actually recognize him. It would be too much of a coincidence if the MVB were not the monogram for Matilda Van Brockhurst, especially as she had similar items of clothing stolen."

"So, he's been stealing from the hand that feeds him?" asked Diane.

"It would seem so but right now, it's my word against his. He's been deceiving her all along. My next call will be to Harry, who will never believe this."

CHAPTER 6

Harry not only believed it, but he also insisted on driving her down to the police station himself. "This case is getting more bizarre by the day," he said. "That poor old woman has been systematically robbed by her own trusted manservant. In my world, it just isn't done."

Lieutenant Balducci wasn't immediately available so they were shown to his office to wait. He came in a few minutes later holding a coffee mug.

"Have you given up licorice, Lieutenant?" teased Veronica.

"Nah," he said. "I asked my wife what was worse . . . dying of lung cancer or dying of sugar diabetes? She said she would rather I died from her nagging. What do you think of that?"

Veronica laughed. "I think she's my kind of woman."

He sat down, folded his arms across his chest, closed his eyes, and said, "Okay, now start at the beginning and tell me your story."

She left nothing out including her visit with Mrs. Van Brockhurst. She mentioned her immediate dislike of Fiske and how she had a bad feeling about him.

Harry put his oar in the water. "Do you think Fiske was the person who sold the goods to Mary and Eddie and the two murder suspects? I can't help but wonder what else is missing from that house."

"I have enough evidence to bring him in for questioning, but if there is someone higher up pulling strings, I don't want to tip my hand just yet."

Harry thought for a moment, then cleared his throat and said, "Well, I could always go for a visit with Veronica the next time she is invited to tea and check things out."

"I don't know if that would be advisable, Mr. Hunt."

"Don't forget, Lieutenant, Mrs. Van Brockhurst lives in my world. In fact, I believe I've heard my mother mention her name and they may have served on some charitable committees together. That connection would be the perfect excuse to gain entry to the house and have a look around without arousing suspicion. As for the butler, well, don't worry. I can handle him. I think the best way for Veronica to proceed is for her to pretend that she never recognized him."

"We have to find out if he's working alone or with someone else," said Veronica. "I can call Mrs. Van Brockhurst tomorrow and suggest she invite us to tea. I know she would welcome the company."

Balducci grudgingly agreed to the plan but cautioned them again to be careful.

Mrs. Van Brockhurst relayed the message to Fiske that she would be delighted to receive a visit from Veronica and Harry and they arranged it for that afternoon. As they drove up the winding cobblestone drive past the four-car garage to the circular front court, they could hear the mournful distant cries of seagulls over the splashing of the fountain. Fiske was already waiting for them beside the massive front door. How different he looks without that silly wig, she thought, while trying to keep a straight face at the memory of it. He ushered them in to the same room and this time Mrs. Van Brockhurst was waiting for them with her nurse. Veronica introduced Harry, and they sat down to tea.

"I believe I know your family, Mr. Hunt," she began. "You are related to the Boston and Newport Hunts?"

"Yes. In fact my mother, Ann, has served on some committees with you and sends her best regards. When I told her I was coming today, she was delighted."

The old lady smiled, nodded, and slowly sipped her tea as the nurse and maid quietly left the room.

"What a beautiful location you have here," said Harry, walking over to the large window wall overlooking the Atlantic Ocean. "Did you build the house or was it in the family?"

"My late husband, Horace, grew up on the North Shore, and after we were married, we only used this house during

July and August. In those days, only two other families were building in the area beside us. He was afraid I would be lonely out here, but we had enough staff to take care of our needs, and I really enjoy the peace and quiet. We had a busy social life at our home in Boston, but I always looked forward to any time spent here by the ocean."

Harry put down his teacup, got up and walked over to the window again. "A beautiful day for sailing," he murmured, admiring the view.

"Horace was commodore of the Bromfield Yacht Club and we spent many happy hours on the water. Fortunately, I have only fond memories of those days. We were not blessed with children, and we spent most of our time in each other's company. We were a very happy couple and were always very comfortable being together so often. I was devastated when I lost him, and I can say truthfully that I miss my husband every day of my life."

Harry and Veronica looked over at each other and smiled. It was not every day that one heard such a ringing endorsement for married life.

"How are you feeling, Mrs. Van Brockhurst?" asked Veronica, breaking the silence. "May I pour you more tea?"

"Yes, thank you, but please call me Mattie. All my friends do."

"If you'll excuse me, I will just find the restroom," said Harry abruptly.

"Tell me about your youth, Mattie," asked Veronica, quickly changing the subject.

"Well, my dear," she began, "I was not born with a silver spoon in my mouth. I was orphaned at a young age and realized early on that I was going to have to look after myself. I was a pretty girl, if I may say it, and after high school decided to follow my dream of going to college. I supported myself with a part-time job as a clerk in a shop that sold exclusive men's clothing. One day Horace came in to buy a shirt. He flirted with me but I didn't encourage him, even though I thought he was amusing.

"He came back the next day for a tie, and the day after that, for some socks. The manager was certain that I was encouraging his advances and warned me that I would be fired if I continued. When Horace came back the next time, I was quite cool to him, and he asked me what the matter was. I explained that I really needed my job. He realized then that he had put my employment in jeopardy. He marched right up to the supervisor and told him he would withdraw his custom immediately if I weren't treated properly. Then he asked me out to dinner for that evening, and I accepted. You could say we had a whirlwind romance."

She paused to sip some tea. Veronica glanced around nervously to see if Fiske had noticed that Harry was no longer in the room.

"My, how we laughed," continued Mattie. "Horace could always make me laugh. I think that's why I fell in love with him. We were secretly married, and when we told his family, they were shocked. I was not what they had in mind for him, of course, but we were always independent thinkers.

That's why we got on so well together. I was able to go to college and get my degree, and he was so proud. I was born a poor girl, but I never let that stop me. Horace indulged me and loved me, and I had a life partner who realized how headstrong I could really be," she giggled.

Soon, Harry slipped back to the room, sat down, and picked up a slice of cake. "Delicious," he announced. "I haven't had a decent piece of seed cake since I can't remember when."

"Mrs. Harris does nice savories as well as having a light hand with pastry," said Mattie. "I'll ring for more cake," she said, reaching for the bell pull.

"I'd like to thank her myself," said Harry, jumping up again. "Would you mind if I went down to the kitchen? I'm sure that I can find my way," he said over his shoulder while hurrying out of the room.

"Harry has a mind of his own," explained Veronica quickly, recognizing that she had Mattie all to herself again. She leaned in and said quietly, "I was wondering and wanted to ask you why a beautiful and valuable diamond ring was sewn into the hem of a coat."

Mattie said nothing for a moment. Then she explained. "We used to travel to Europe quite a bit in those days, and travel by ship could be a little dangerous. My maid at the time suggested we hide some of my jewels in unlikely places as she never trusted anyone who spoke a foreign language. I would have my fittings in Paris at Mademoiselle Chanel's and at Paul Poiret's atelier, and when they finished, my gowns were delivered to the hotel. Daisy would pack them in steamer trunks after sewing various pieces of my jewelry into the hems for safekeeping. I had quite forgotten the ring was still there. I suppose I should make sure there are no others."

"Would you like me to help you, Mattie? It would be my pleasure, really," said Veronica, realizing this was the perfect excuse to come back again.

"It would be like a little treasure hunt, wouldn't it, my dear? Oh, what fun we will have."

"Let's just keep this between ourselves, shall we? I can come back tomorrow, if that's all right, and we can get started. It will be our little secret." She winked at the old lady and got a conspiring smile in return.

Harry came back in the room then and said he had obtained the cook's recipe for her seed cake. "It was the only thing I enjoyed eating at boarding school. We will not bother you any longer, Mattie. Thank you for the tea, and I'll be sure to give your best wishes to my mother."

Veronica gave him a quick glance and wondered why he was suggesting such a quick departure. Fiske appeared and ushered them to the door. He stared straight ahead and intoned a stony "good afternoon" at their retreating figures.

"Isn't he a real barrel of laughs?" observed Harry, getting behind the wheel of the Porsche. "I'm positive he followed me down to the kitchen, but I made sure I doubled back up the stairs before I had a good look around."

Veronica told him about tomorrow's plans. "I have all I

can do to keep myself from laughing when I picture him in that blond wig. No one can ever say he makes an attractive woman."

"Let's call Balducci and give him a report, then figure out how to proceed tomorrow. Just a reminder too that we are having dinner tonight at the Grill On The Waterfront with the gang. I'll pick you up at 6:00."

"I forgot all about it, Harry. Do we have to go?"

"It's Bunny's birthday celebration, so, yes, we have to go. Her best friend from college is flying in from L.A., and that makes seven of us for dinner. It'll be fun."

To her mind, Harry's friends, or "gang," as he referred to them, were anything *but* fun. They constantly complained about the search to find the right servants, recounted the myriad petty squabbles at their clubs, and moaned about their children's school tuitions. She sighed deeply and steeled herself for an evening of sacrifice on the altar of love and friendship.

CHAPTER 7

Justine Palmer was not having an easy time of it. At the time of his death, Earl had left her with nothing but bills. She found out shortly after they married that he was a thief, pure and simple. When she became aware that his day job as a jeweler was more or less a cover, she was shocked and disgusted. Earl was trained in diamond setting, making and designing custom jewelry, soldering, and intricate repair work, and he was good at it. When they were dating, she was under the impression that he had a good trade that would always be in demand. He owned a small shop with a modest inventory, and his repair work for other jewelers always kept him busy and paid the bills.

Then she learned that he was also a well-known fence for stolen jewelry. The veneer of respectability that she had always craved was going to take a lot of work to retain, and she steeled herself for a long road ahead. He had deceived her, and she would have to make the best of the situation. While he was alive, and as long as he brought home enough money to give her a good life, she had turned a blind eye. Her lifelong obsession with jewelry was the chief reason she married him in the first place. She told herself that now she would be able to own rather than covet beautiful jewelry, but the trade-off was that she would just have to live with his little sideline.

Justine was considered a good-looking woman. She had thick, dark brown hair with lighter highlights worn in a shoulder-length layered cut, and her busty figure drew many admiring glances from men who wanted to know her better. She was careful to dress in clothing that enhanced her assets, and she was rather partial to designer labels.

Her secret was that she had a tough childhood. Her widowed mother had to work hard as a cleaning lady at two jobs to support Justine and her brother John. While she was still in grade school, a physical exam revealed a rheumatic heart condition. Her mother was cautioned to keep an eye on her, but her willful daughter did not want to be excluded from anything because of a disability or to call attention to any weakness, physical or otherwise. Justine didn't believe in weakness of any kind. She always wanted to present a face to the world that was upbeat, happy, and carefree. It was also important to the young girl that she have a strong male role model; a man who worked hard, protected his family, and who could afford to give her the pretty things she craved. Unfortunately, her father had died when Justine was still very young, and she never forgave him for leaving her alone and in her mind, abandoned.

All her school friends dressed in the latest styles and always seemed to have money to buy cosmetics and jewelry, things that matter to a young and impressionable girl. When they flaunted their latest possessions, she made a show of being happy for them, but secretly, she was seething with jealousy. Her personality was always upbeat and positive, and few knew her well enough to be able to identify the steely, no-nonsense resolve that drove her in everything she did.

Justine had grown up quickly and she made a pact with herself that she would own the things in her adult life that she couldn't possibly afford as a young girl. And why not? she reasoned. I don't always feel well, and I should be able to be like my friends who have fathers to talk to and mothers who don't have to work all the time.

Then Earl began to bring home the jewelry he and his friends had stolen. They were magnificent, wonderful pieces that she would give anything to own; her old insecurities always boiling below the surface. Her jewelry fetish wouldn't be satisfied because she couldn't have them. The gold had to be melted down and scrapped for its weight, and the stones were sold to other jewelers to make their creations. Sure, the money came in handy, and she was able to buy nice clothes and take vacations in warm climates, but it broke her heart to see such beautiful jewelry destroyed and broken apart when she could be wearing it herself. She could be basking in the glory of seeing jealous glances from other women.

Wearing stolen jewelry in public was out of the question, of course. "What if the rightful owner ever saw you wearing them, Justine?" argued Earl. "Don't be a silly bitch. We can't take any chances like that." She knew he was making sense, but she just couldn't get it out of her mind, and he couldn't seem to understand that she wanted to own the jewelry she could never afford, just like when she was young.

Justine had worked as the private secretary to the vice president of the Bromfield Trust before her marriage and was able to get her old job back after Earl was killed. She had earned the respect of her fellow workers, and her boss, a longtime employee of the bank, relied on her to run his private life too after his wife had recently died following a long-term illness. Justine was quite sure now that Mr. Daniels couldn't live without her. She was secretly in love with him, and she was confident that he felt the same about her.

He relied on her for everything and said so constantly. She saw to it that all his bills were paid, that he never forgot his married daughter's birthday, remembered when his yearly car inspection sticker was due, made sure his club memberships and doctors' appointments were up to date—all in addition to her responsibilities at the office. He always told her he would be lost without her and that he depended on her to see that his life ran smoothly. He praised her ability to keep all the balls in the air while making sure the corporate side of his life ran like clockwork.

One day he asked her to stop by the cleaners after lunch and pick up a suit and deliver it to his home. He wouldn't have time to do it himself, of course, because he had some important paperwork to catch up on. When she arrived at his house, the back door was open, and she decided to hang the suit in the hall closet. As she was about to leave, she heard noises coming from the family room. The surprised look on Mr. Daniels's face when she walked in on him and the teenage daughter of the senior teller rolling around on the carpet in their underwear was nothing compared to the pained expression on Justine's face. She shrieked and ran out the door as fast as her high heels would take her.

How could he do this to me? she fumed. How could he deceive me? Where would he be without me, without my help in running his life? He wasn't much to look at, she had to admit, but he had everything Earl did not—respectability, a secure and steady income, the approval of his peers, status in the community—all the things she wanted too. This betrayal was too much.

She decided then and there that it was time to take matters into her own hands. When she calmed down and thought about it, she reasoned that this situation could work in her favor if she took her hurt feelings and disappointment out of the equation. She now had the goods on David Daniels, and with a little planning and patience, she could make it work to her advantage. For once she had the upper hand and she wasn't going to relinquish it for anyone or anything. He would pay for his betrayal and deception, and she had no problem with seeing him squirm; in fact, she looked forward to it. If he thought she ran his life before, then he hadn't seen anything yet. How dare he throw her over for a teenage Lolita?

She contacted Harry, Louie, and her brother John and met them in a coffee shop several miles from town. They were curious about why the woman who always treated them like dirt whenever they came to her and Earl's house had summoned them to a meeting. Justine wasted no time in coming to the point. She wanted them to resume their old business with her as the new partner.

They looked at her as if she were a madwoman, talking in tongues.

She told them she wanted in and pointed out that she was an expert in the planning and the execution of details. She made a case for her involvement, and when they finally laughed at her plan, she threatened them with exposure. They hadn't yet realized that she was not going to take no for an answer.

"The police already know about us," sneered Harry. "Didn't you see them at the funeral watching us like hawks?"

"Yeah," said Louie. "We're thinking of moving the operation somewhere else until things cool off around here, so we don't really need your help."

She pressed on. "In case you don't realize it, I'm still the private secretary to the vice president of the Bromfield Bank & Trust."

"So what?" challenged Louie.

John, never slow in recognizing an opportunity, spoke up. "In case you morons don't get it, what my sister is telling you is that she has an 'in' at the bank."

They remained silent as the waitress delivered their

coffee and donuts order to the table.

Justine resumed. "I have a lot more than just an 'in.' I have information and I have keys and codes. I know times, dates, and have access to log books. And, most importantly, I have the complete cooperation of my boss, who owes me big time."

Three heads slowly wagged in the affirmative while digesting this information. The possibilities were beginning to become clear to them.

But what Justine didn't know at the time was that Harold and Louie were working jobs on their own that didn't necessarily involve just jewelry theft. They had formed a close association with another mastermind.

CHAPTER 8

It was a beautiful summer evening in Boston, perfect for a birthday celebration at an exceptionally fine seafood restaurant on the waterfront, but Veronica was not in a celebratory mood. She hardly knew Bunny and wondered why a grown woman would call herself by such a childish name. In fact, the last time they met, the waiter had accidentally spilled a glass of wine on Bunny's designer dress and she seemed to think it was all Veronica's fault because she had asked him a question about the menu at precisely the same moment he answered, which distracted him, and the accident happened.

But for the sake of Harry, she put on a happy face. She dressed in a vintage red sheath dress that molded her body perfectly. Her ridiculously high heels were the same red shoes she was wearing the day she met Harry and knew they were his favorite. The dress stopped just above her knees, showing her long legs to their best advantage. Not bad, she thought, looking at her reflection in the bedroom mirror. She was always her own best critic, but tonight, she had nothing to criticize except the company she was being forced to keep. They all met at the bar and two bottles of champagne later, she made up for the insincere handshake she gave the birthday girl when they arrived. "Congratulations, Barbara," said Veronica, "and many happy returns of the day."

Bunny's former college roommate, Sandra, was introduced, and she immediately latched on to Harry, taking his arm and steering him toward the window overlooking the harbor. She monopolized him for a good part of the evening and made no effort to disguise her blatant efforts to flirt. She's a bit old to be batting her eyelashes, thought Veronica. Sure, she has a nice figure (though rather obvious in that low-cut white dress that shows quite a bit of cleavage) and lovely blond hair with expensive highlights, but she must surely realize that Harry is with me.

When their table was ready, she took the bull by the horns and marched over to them, kissed Harry on the cheek, and pointedly announced, "Darling, it's time to stop bothering Sandra and sit down to dinner." She pulled him to the seat next to her at the end of the table. Sandra had no choice but to sit at the opposite end, being the odd-numbered guest.

They all started with oysters on the half shell. More champagne arrived, and the appetizer dish she shared with Harry featured stuffed clams, fried calamari rings with a citrus dipping sauce and scallops wrapped in bacon, all so delicious that it almost made her ignore the fact that Sandra was shooting daggers at her from the other end of the table. Beef Wellington followed with haricot verts and roasted potatoes, and for dessert, the chef's birthday creation, his award-winning version of strawberry shortcake.

They ate to bursting and their laughter was contagious. Veronica found she was really enjoying herself in spite of the rocky start. Live music started up in the lounge and they all drifted to the bar for a nightcap. Sandra saw an opportunity to take Harry by the hand and drag him on to the dance floor for a slow dance then she plastered herself against him. He tried to pull away but couldn't do so gracefully and tactfully because a pro was handling him, so he just smiled and enjoyed the dance.

Veronica looked around and caught Bunny winking at Sandra. This is a set up, she thought, pure and simple. Well, we'll see about that. When the music stopped, they kept on dancing, this time to a slow fox trot. Veronica sashayed over, tapped Sandra on the shoulder, and loudly announced, "I'm cutting in," then eased her aside with a sharp movement of her hip. After a few minutes, she whispered in his ear. "You can wipe that smirk off your face, Harry Hunt. No one's going to steal my guy tonight."

Harry was a good dancer because young men of his class always took lessons. He glided her around the floor and held her especially tight and knew he was enjoying this evening more than he could say. It had been some time since two beautiful women fought over him, and he was relishing the attention. After all the good-byes were said, Sandra retired defeated, knowing that Bunny's plan wasn't going to work after all.

On the drive home it was Harry who brought up the

antics of the obvious Sandra. "Don't apologize, Harry," cooed Veronica. "It was all planned by Bunny and executed by Sandra. You were just a pawn in the game." Her words immediately deflated his ego and he was momentarily speechless. She reached over and patted his hand and said, "Don't worry, dear; men are always the last to know."

CHAPTER 9

The plan was that Veronica would go back to the mansion the next day and go through Mattie's closets and look for any more jewelry sewn in the hems. She would keep an eye out for Fiske and make sure she had Mattie's complete attention while she searched. Veronica and Harry agreed not to tell her yet that Fiske was responsible for the robberies and that he was selling her belongings at a flea market.

Veronica arrived with a large tote bag containing scissors, a jeweler's loupe, a camera, notebook, and her ubiquitous harlequin eyeglasses. She was shown upstairs by the maid who walked her to Mattie's large bedroom overlooking the sea. Mattie greeted her in the wheelchair, holding a beautiful white angora cat on her lap. "This is Fiona, my baby," she said, stroking her fur.

The room was a vision in shades of pink. The curtains were cream silk with tiny pink rosebuds and green fernery and matched the bedspread and tufted headboard and footboard. A bench at the foot of the bed was covered in the same fabric. The gilt wood canopy surrounding the bed had draperies of cream and pale pink silk stripes that matched the pillows on the bed. The room was hung with Impressionist paintings, and a group of French botanical prints was displayed over the dressing table which contained several large perfume bottles and cut glass jars. A French Aubusson carpet of cream and rose covered most of the floor.

"This is my girly girl room," explained Mattie, "and I never get tired of looking at it. It's not the largest bedroom in the house, but it gets the morning sun first."

Veronica thought she too would be very happy in this room, morning light or no light.

Mattie handed Fiona to the maid and said she would ring if she needed anything. Veronica watched her leave then walked over to the large carved walnut wardrobe at the end of the room and asked if they should start there.

"Oh no," she giggled. "This isn't my closet. My closet is through there," and she pointed to a connecting door. Veronica wheeled her through the doorway which revealed another huge room lined with shelving from the floor to the ceiling containing shoes, handbags, hats, dresses, gowns, sportswear, coats, and jackets, all filed away according to the seasons and color coded. A cedar lined closet contained furs of every description.

Veronica's eyes bulged at the sight. "How many pair of shoes do you own, Mattie?"

"I never counted them, dear."

"Imelda Marcos has nothing on you," she quipped, looking around.

A large alcove closet with walls entirely mirrored in glass was where the vintage clothing reposed. A bench and dressing table centered the room and Veronica started laying various items on them at Mattie's direction. Dozens of beautifully preserved pieces came out, each housed in its own cloth bag. It was like Christmas morning for Veronica. She was able to see and hold gowns made by the top names in Parisian couture of the Art Deco period. Mattie recited amusing anecdotes for each dress and remembered being fitted for most of them.

"Dear Coco fitted me personally for that," she said, pointing to a bias cut crepe number in aubergine silk. "She accidentally pricked me with a pin, and when I said 'Ouch,' she told me she wouldn't charge me extra for the Band-Aid. She was tough as nails, that one, but oh, she could design gowns that made you look so slim and chic."

Out came another model, this one in silver lame with a low cowl neckline in front and backless. "I wore that to a New Year's Eve party at the Vanderbilts' in London. Everyone was there. The Duchess of Windsor asked me if Schiaparelli designed my dress. I said to her, 'Wallis, you do have an eye for clothes.' She winked and said she also had an eye for men as well, and flicked her cigarette holder in the general direction of the future king of England."

Veronica was enchanted with the stories and the woman telling them. "What about this one?" she asked and held up a patterned blue silk velvet chemise with a black chiffon handkerchief hem.

"That's another Chanel model. I wore it to a birthday party in Cannes. Let me see, oh yes, I remember now. Horace said it reminded him of some draperies his mother had. When I told him how much Chanel charged for it, he choked. Well," she mused, "at least the king of Romania liked it. He said I reminded him of a lovely sea nymph."

Veronica sat down on the bench and felt along the hem. She picked up her scissors and began to take out some tiny stitches. "Success!" she cried and pulled out a pair of sapphire and diamond chandelier earrings.

Mattie's eyes bulged when she saw them. "I forgot I had those! I wore them with the gown that night. My maid certainly went overboard, didn't she?" Veronica wondered if Mattie would even know what was missing from her closet after all these years. Because she had so much, even Fiske wasn't aware that some of the things he had stolen had diamonds and precious stones sewn into the hems. She was more determined than ever to bring this despicable man to justice.

They spent the rest of the morning just going through the vintage clothing closet until every item was piled up on the bench. Veronica found three more hidden pieces of jewelry: a large and beautiful emerald and diamond ring with the matching earrings hidden in another hem and a large sapphire, amethyst, and gold pin in the shape of a basket of flowers, this item hiding in a pair of pale pink leather, elbow length, opera gloves.

"Can you think of any piece of jewelry that has gone missing recently?" asked Veronica, putting the clothing back in the closet.

Mattie thought a moment and said that now that she mentioned it, she couldn't remember seeing her particular favorite, a diamond watch from Cartier, lately. "It was an anniversary present from Horace. The dial is so small, and my eyes aren't what they used to be, but I treasure it just the same. I asked my maid, but she couldn't remember seeing it either."

"Tell me about your maid. Has she been with you awhile?"

"Ivy has been my maid for about three years now, and I trust her as much as I trust Fiske."

Veronica didn't say anything and filed away this information in her head. "I suggest we hide the jewelry we found today and tell no one about it, not even Ivy." There was a wall safe behind one of the paintings in the bedroom and Mattie remembered the combination.

She then rang for Ivy and asked her to tell Cook that a guest was staying for luncheon. Veronica saw the maid's eyes dart around the room before she left on her errand. She was a nondescript-looking woman, small and wiry, in her middle forties, with short, mousy-brown hair and a slightly hooked nose. She reminded Veronica of a ferret.

Lunch was served under an awning that surrounded the stone patio. It was a beautiful, warm day with a slight breeze. The old-fashioned wrought iron table and chairs were large and comfortable, and the glass top reflected the sunlight. The table was set with oversized, white crisp linen monogrammed napkins, sterling flatware, and cut crystal

glasses. The patio looked out over the rocks and the mani-
cured lawn that sloped down to the water's edge. The menu
was simple: quiche Lorraine, a garden salad, and a crusty
loaf of French bread. "I have to admit to a sweet tooth," said
Mattie, "so I asked Cook to make my favorite dessert today,
a Charlotte Russe." Fiske served silently at the table while
they ate in companionable silence, enjoying the beautiful
day and delicious food.

At one point Mattie asked, "I don't mean to be personal,
dear, but did you never marry?"

"No," answered Veronica, "I never seemed to have the
time or inclination. I had my work and my dream to open a
store, and the Boston fellows I'd dated had not really been
husband material. I guess I'm a loner at heart."

"What about Mr. Hunt?" she twinkled. "In my day, he
would have been called a 'good catch.' A nice, cultured gen-
tleman from a good family who is obviously fond of you is
not so bad, is it?"

"Harry is more like a good friend to me, really."

"Take it from me, dear, that's how the best marriages
start. You have to be friends first."

They continued to eat in silence, and she took the opportunity to observe Mattie enjoying her dessert. Here was
a wise woman who had everything life had to offer and she
relished every minute. She was a true lady, a sweet and
cultured woman, and her generation and station in life dic-
tated that one didn't make waves. Her late husband always
protected her. Dating advice apart, she was obviously not

someone who held a grudge and trusted people who have ended up taking advantage of her. She had no other family, and now, there was nobody left to keep her safe.

Veronica decided then and there to become Mattie's advocate, to bring all the people responsible for robbing her to justice. Yes, she was outraged that beautiful objects were being sold for a fraction of their value, but even more importantly, Mattie's trust was being violated, and that really bothered her more than anything.

In many ways, Matilda Van Brockhurst reminded her of Aunt Gillian. Their spunk and spirit and wisdom were the same and they were both independent thinkers at a time when women were frowned upon if they spoke up for their rights.

Veronica vowed to do whatever it took to bring down Fiske and his cohorts. Murder was committed to obtain beautiful baubles, and greed always seemed to propel these people. She couldn't stand the idea that a lovely, elderly woman was being taken advantage of in such a blatant manner.

As she was preparing to leave, she whispered again to Mattie to trust no one and reminded her that until the police could give them further information about who murdered Eddie and who robbed her, they still had to be vigilant.

She promised to return soon and Mattie took her hand and squeezed it. "I had a wonderful day, and I appreciate all your help."

CHAPTER 10

The shop's tinkling doorbell told Veronica she had a customer, and Lieutenant Balducci walked in.

"Well, well! To what do I owe the honor of a visit from one of Bromfield's most illustrious chief homicide detectives?"

"You mean Bromfield's *only* illustrious chief homicide detective," he said, looking around. "Nice little place you've got here, Miss Howard. My wife and daughter would enjoy shopping here."

"Tell them to come in, Lieutenant. I can always use the business."

"Let's go over there and talk," he suggested, walking to the back of the store and sitting down on a cane chair.

"In return for a plea bargain, we got some information that you should know about from the two suspects. Those bozos say they are working for a boss, whose name they don't know, who is organizing systematic thefts from rich, elderly, and infirm people like your Mrs. Van Brockhurst.

"It seems that the stolen items won't be missed as they are snatched over a long period, stashed somewhere, then sold at flea markets. We already check the local pawn shops regularly, but the culprits are too smart to try to unload them there."

"Do you believe their story, Lieutenant? I mean why would they steal valuable things and then sell them at a flea market for a fraction of their worth, and over a long time? It doesn't make sense to me. And they didn't even know the really valuable stuff is sewn into the hems of garments."

Balducci reached into his jacket pocket and pulled out a licorice stick. "You know you've got a good point about not knowing about what things are worth." He took the wrapper off the candy and put it in his mouth.

"What flavor is this one?"

"Strawberry." He chewed awhile, then said, "There's got to be more to this. We're missing something here."

Suddenly she jumped up, walked around her desk with her hands on her hips, and stood in front of him. "What if they are getting the poor old souls to sign over their entire estates in their wills?"

He chewed thoughtfully. "We haven't received any complaints of that nature, but I suppose it's possible."

"Mrs. Van Brockhurst has no heirs as she and her husband were childless," Veronica explained. "She is elderly and depends on her nurse and servants. But her mind is still sharp and she would probably question it if someone suggested changing her will in their favor. I need to ask her if anything like that has ever come up.

"Lieutenant, I have to get her out of that house for a few hours on some pretext and ask her these questions. Also, she has to know that Fiske has been robbing her over a long time. We at least owe that to her."

"I suggest we keep that information under our hats for a little while longer, Miss Howard, at least until we find out who is fronting this operation. We can't afford to tip our hand too soon."

"Would you object if Harry and I took her for an afternoon out and at least asked her if anything suspicious has been going on? She can't really talk in that house because the walls have ears."

"That's a good idea. We need more information about who is running the show, and Mrs. Van Brockhurst trusts you."

CHAPTER 11

To keep fit and help her wind down, Veronica joined a yoga group at the Bromfield Public Library. She had given a lecture on vintage clothing for them some months before and liked the friendly staff. The yoga class was held in a sunny room hung with cheerful watercolors painted by a local artist.

The instructor greeted her with a smile and a hug. "I'm glad you could join us today, Veronica."

"Thanks, Dale. You know how much I look forward to your class all week."

An hour later, as she was rolling up her mat, she overheard two women discussing the bargains they had found at the flea market the previous Sunday. They were both collectors of fine glass and each had found a valuable signed vase, one by Tiffany and one by René Lalique. They described the booth holder as a blonde with an abrupt manner.

Sounds as if Fiske is still up to his old tricks, she thought, and went back to the store to phone Harry. She also reported her conversation with Balducci.

"I have an idea," said Harry. "Call Mattie and tell her my mother wants to invite her to tea to discuss the old days, an excellent excuse to get her out of that house. We can ask her about her will and if the maid knows the combination to the safe."

Veronica immediately called the mansion, and Fiske answered. She was told that Madame was not able to come to the phone as she was indisposed. When she pressed him for details, he evaded her questions and suggested she call back the next day. She hung up the phone feeling suddenly alarmed and called Harry back.

"She seemed fine the other day, Harry. I don't have a good feeling about this at all. Fiske and that maid run her life, and if they think we're getting close to the truth, they will say or do anything to keep us at arm's length."

"I'll come to Bromfield this afternoon, and we'll drive over there together and push our way in, if we have to. Don't worry; we'll get to the bottom of this. I've grown fond of the old girl and don't like what they are doing to her any more than you do."

When Harry pulled up in the Porsche, she noticed a large basket of fruit in the backseat. "Just a little insurance policy," he said, answering her inquiring glance.

When they got to the mansion, Fiske opened the door after some minutes. He looked at them both, then at the fruit basket Harry was holding and back again with a dead stare.

"We're so sorry to hear Mrs. Van Brockhurst is under the weather and want to cheer her up with this," chirped Veronica, pointing to the basket.

"I'm afraid the doctor won't allow visitors, miss, but I'll make sure that she receives your gift," and he reached for the basket.

Thinking quickly, she added, "I'm also here to pick up my prescription glasses that I left behind the other day. I really need them, Fiske," she said firmly. "We will just wait inside while you look for them."

He blinked a couple of times, defeated, and stood aside while they filed in. Harry shoved the basket at him and they walked directly to the morning room. Presently the maid, Ivy, came in. "I'm sorry, miss, but I couldn't find your glasses anywhere. Are you sure you left them here?"

"I'm sure I did and you can't miss them. They're bright red, and they turn up at the corners. They may be in Mrs. Van Brockhurst's dressing room on the bench."

"I looked there, miss, and didn't see them," she said firmly.

"I know that's the last place I had them. Why don't I just pop up and have a look myself," Veronica said, and she marched toward the staircase, taking her handbag with her. Harry followed her with the maid trailing behind them, wailing that Madame could not possibly receive any visitors.

They arrived at Mattie's room and saw the old lady lying in bed, hair disheveled and skin color not the healthy pink of the other day but blotchy and slightly sallow. Her eyes were closed and her breathing was ragged. The curtains were drawn and gloom pervaded the formerly bright and cheerful space. Veronica rushed to her side and took her pulse.

It was uneven, and as she glanced at the bedside table, she saw an array of medicine bottles and a syringe on a tray.

"Has the doctor been called?" she asked Ivy while walking over to open the curtains to let in the light.

Then Fiske came in and surveyed the scene. "Begging your pardon, miss, but we don't have to answer your questions. You are not related to Mrs. Van Brockhurst. *We* are her family, and we have everything under control."

While he was talking, Harry discreetly snapped pictures of Fiske and Ivy with a hidden camera.

"We have become friends, Fiske, and frankly, Miss Howard and I are not satisfied that you are doing everything you can to help her," said Harry stepping in front of the butler. "I would like the doctor's name, please, so we can satisfy ourselves that she is getting the best care."

Mattie stirred a little on the bed, and Veronica rushed over to her side. "Mattie," she said, taking the old lady's hand. "Mattie, can you hear me?" Mattie opened her eyes, stared at Veronica, and smiled.

"Hello, dear," she whispered. "Shall I ring for tea?"

Veronica could see that her pupils were dilated. Those bastards are drugging her!

CHAPTER 12

After she discovered him having sex with the teenage daughter of an employee, David Daniels became putty in Justine's hands. She made it clear that she would blow the whistle on him if he got in her way or questioned her new authority. She held all the cards now, and the power she possessed was intoxicating. He promised to give up his young paramour after admitting he had been meeting her secretly for about a month after admiring her at the company picnic.

Justine began formulating a plan in her head for Earl's old gang to rob the bank. She had found out just before Earl was killed that he was also acting as a fence for other jewelry robberies around the state. He had kept that information hidden from her as well as the profits. Now she was going to make up for his tricks by figuring out how to do it herself. Her bank salary paid the mortgage, car payments, food, and her heart medicine, but very little else. The opportunity was there; she just had to put a plan in place. She was good at planning and she could be sitting pretty very soon if she played her cards right.

She re-thought her fixation with Daniels. Why would she

want to saddle herself with another weak man when she could have a whole new and different life? She reasoned that once she accumulated enough cash, she would be able to move to a warmer climate and find a real man, someone who appreciated a beautiful woman who wore beautiful jewelry. She would make an appointment with a plastic surgeon and have a little nip and tuck. A new wardrobe would quickly follow and also a smart new car; one of those sporty two-seaters in bright red so she would stand out in a crowd.

Yes, her time had come, and she was going to grab every opportunity with both hands. Daniels would provide her with information on the customers he knew who had expensive jewelry in their vaults. He knew them socially and could fill her in on their movements . . . when they went on vacation to their second homes and when they planned on making big purchases through bank loans. She would then figure out several scenarios and present them to Harold, Louie, and her brother John for execution. Yes, things were finally coming together now and she would ensure that her plans were carried out to her specifications by the others.

Justine looked in the mirror and saw a new and different woman staring back. Her days of being quiet and compliant were now behind her. The insecurities she had suffered by being poor and sickly in her youth were going to disappear, starting now. She realized that she had been given a chance to reshape her life, and the talents she possessed were going to provide her with the catalyst to move on. What did she care who got hurt along the way? Did anyone give a second thought to her feelings when she was growing up?

Once in a while, when Earl had too much to drink and was feeling particularly morose, he would lash out and hit her. She would come in to work with bruises that she was able to cover up with long sleeves, but once he gave her a black eye. She made up a story that she had tripped and fallen down the stairs that no one seemed to question.

Then one day a co-worker happened to comment on her bruised eye. The woman confided that her husband drank and occasionally beat her too. Justine turned on her and told her she was mistaken; her husband wouldn't dare do that to her. The woman just looked at her with pity in her eyes, patted her on the wrist, and said she would always be available to listen if Justine wanted to get anything off her chest. Imagine, the nerve of her, thought Justine.

Why would anyone think that I was like her, a miserable little mealy-mouth; the victim of an out-of-control husband? That night in bed, though, the tears wouldn't stop as she remembered the woman's words and kind offer of kinship. Justine hadn't fooled everyone with her story.

CHAPTER 13

There was nothing to be gained by having a Mexican standoff with the butler and maid, so Veronica and Harry left the mansion and immediately drove to the station house to look for the lieutenant. As he listened to their story, Harry pulled out the camera to show him the pictures he had taken. Balducci punched the intercom button and Officer Anderson came in.

"Run these two through our files, will you, Anderson, and see what you come up with. It won't surprise me if they both have records."

He turned to them and said, "Good job to you both. Mrs. Van Brockhurst was drugged, you say?"

"Yes, Lieutenant, and her pulse wasn't steady," said Veronica. "I saw a syringe on the bedside table, and I also saw the physician's name on the label of one of the vials, a Dr. Slattery."

"That fraud!" cried Balducci. "I wouldn't let him take care of my dog if I had one. How did you leave things at the house?"

"We reluctantly walked out," said Harry, "and hated leaving her there with those two leeches."

Two cups of coffee each later and Anderson came back in.

"Bingo," said Officer Anderson and smiled. "Fiske is really Pavlo Sidlauski, and Ivy is Wilhelmina Dugan, both wanted by the Chicago P.D. for confidence swindles and embezzlement targeted at rich, old folks. Sounds kinda familiar, doesn't it?"

"Attaboy, that's what I'm talking about!" cried Balducci punching the air. "Let's get a warrant out for their arrest, now!"

An hour later, three unmarked squad cars, one unmarked police van and one Porsche sports car wound their way up the hill to the Van Brockhurst mansion. Even though it was now early dusk, there were no lights on. They pounded on the door and after a minute or two the bulky figure of the cook appeared in the doorway, eyes like saucers. She said that Fiske and Ivy had taken Madame away in the car, saying they wouldn't be back until later that night. They all rushed upstairs, only to find an empty bedroom and house.

Balducci called the station to get an address for Dr. Slattery. "Might as well start there," he said.

The doctor had offices at his home and when they pulled up, one light was on in the front window. A woman in a lab coat answered the doorbell and advised that the doctor had just left for a house call. She looked up the address in her appointment book and said it was down on the waterfront at the rear of a gift shop. The patient was a retired ship captain who ran the shop and lived upstairs. Yes, she said, she was sure he had a boat.

A call for backup resulted in two more unmarked police cars going to the same address. A sign on the door indicated that the shop was closed for business until further notice.

Veronica and Harry were instructed to stay in the car while several officers surrounded the gift shop. "What are we going to do if they have killed her, Harry, or have tried to take her away by boat? This waiting here in the car is killing me."

"Let's not get carried away, Veronica. Mattie is no good to them dead. They need her signature and she is worth more to them alive. Let's pray the police have gotten to them in time and that she has been able to hold on."

The raid was carried out with silence and precision. The officers broke the door down and surprised Fiske, Ivy, Dr. Slattery, and Captain Matlock in a dirty upstairs room where they were preparing another dose of drugs to inject her with. They were handcuffed and loaded into the police van. Mattie was safely retrieved from a cot in an advanced drugged state and taken immediately to Bromfield General Hospital.

They had in their possession papers that would change Mattie's will in favor of her butler and maid. Fortunately, she had not signed, and they could only guess to what length these criminals were willing to go through to gain access to her entire estate. The needle tracks in her arms along with the bruises on her body gave them an idea of the criminals' resolve and how close they were to obtaining their goal.

Two days after she was found, the hospital allowed visitors. A pale and weak Mattie was sitting up in bed, an intravenous hooked up to her arm and an oxygen tube in her nose, when Veronica and Harry arrived. She was sufficiently alert and able to recognize her visitors. She had been made aware that she was still alive because of the quick action of the two people sitting by her bed.

"I'll always be grateful to you both," she whispered. "I never thought anyone could take advantage of me like that, and I'm so disappointed in them and ashamed of myself for believing their stories. Thank you for looking after me," she said slowly, it clearly being an effort to speak. They stayed with her in the room, holding her hands until she fell asleep.

Veronica left the hospital clinging to Harry's arm and with tears in her eyes. "Buck up, dearest," he said. "The story could have had a very different ending, you know."

"I hope they throw the book at those creeps. We'll come back again in a few days when Mattie feels better."

CHAPTER 14

Saturday was always a busy day at Veronica's Vintage, and later in the afternoon, when business started to slow a little, Diane came in and introduced the idea of another trip to the flea market to a reluctant Veronica.

"Come on, Ronnie," she said, glancing around the store. "It looks like you could use a break and a chance to buy some more items to sell. I mean, it's not as if you're going to be bumping into Fiske again, is it?" she laughed.

"No, and thank goodness he's out of the picture and behind bars along with that other nasty piece of work, Ivy."

"How is Mrs. Van Brockhurst feeling?"

"She's home now with her full-time nurse and looking and feeling one hundred percent better. I'm amazed at how resilient she is and put it down to her zest for life. No one should be allowed to go through what she experienced, at any age."

"Well, thanks to you, Harry, and the Bromfield Police Department, she never will have to go through anything like that again. I'm sure she knows she's lucky to be alive." They made a date to get an early start the next morning with Diane driving.

Another beautiful day dawned, and the parking lot was almost full when they pulled in around 7:30 a.m. They wore their flea market "uniforms" of rubber-soled shoes, jeans, light layers of clothing, sun hats, and tote bags. About two hundred dealers were set up, and some had small, make-shift tents in front of their cars for shade, anticipating the hot day ahead.

Up and down the aisles they went, stopping only for a coffee and a donut after an hour. It felt good to sit, and it was then that Veronica experienced that odd tingle down her spine. She said nothing to Diane about it. She recognized a few of her customers walking around, collectors and devotees like herself, of vintage clothing. Occasionally, the roar of a Harley Davidson motorcycle could be heard as the annual summer gathering of local motorcycle clubs was being held about five miles up the road. Someone was strumming a guitar, and the baby carriages and dog walkers were out in full strength on this beautiful summer morning.

Veronica was able to find some interesting pieces of jewelry that would pair well with the clothing she sold. She found she could make multiple sales when she suggested an appropriate pair of period earrings or a vintage necklace to go with an outfit. Her customers trusted her judgment and taste.

They had already made a trip back to the car to drop off purchases and decided to walk one more time around the back field where a few new dealers were late in setting up their booths. One man was hammering in the last pole of his tent, and the shade was attracting customers. There was a blanket on the ground with various clothing items piled up, and Ronnie went over to investigate.

Out of the corner of her eye, she spotted a pleated velvet jacket that looked very much like the one Mattie owned. She made a beeline for the pile and pulled it out. She couldn't believe that she was holding a Chinese-influenced 1920's jacket, and upon further inspection, she was astonished to see the "MVB" monogram embroidered on the inside seam. She called Diane to come quickly and showed her. They stared at each other, then looked up at the dealer to ask for a price.

Veronica almost fainted as Fiske stared back at them, only this time he wasn't wearing a blond wig. He was his natural gaunt looking, bald self.

"May I help you ladies?" he asked, his pointed wolf like teeth showing in a rictus grin. She held on to Diane's arm to keep her knees from buckling under and suddenly, she couldn't find her voice.

He acted as if he had never seen her before. "It's a nice jacket, isn't it, and I'm pretty sure it's an antique. You seem to know what you want, so I'll make you a lot price if you buy any of the other items there," he said pointing to the blanket.

She nodded wordlessly and walked over to where he was pointing as he started to wait on another customer. Diane leaned over, pretending to look too, and asked her what she was going to do.

"I can't understand how he can be standing here as clear as daylight; he's supposed to be in jail," said Veronica through clenched teeth. "He's either the best actor in the world, or he really doesn't recognize us."

She looked back and studied him again. He seemed a little taller than she remembered and there was gray stubble on his chin. He had the same pointed teeth, but somehow, he was slightly different. Then it dawned on her.

"He's a twin, Diane, an identical twin! I'm sure of it now." They both turned at the same time and stared.

"But what's he doing here selling Mattie's clothing? I thought Fiske was the ringleader, and we know for sure that he's in jail."

"We have to pretend we don't recognize him and play along," she hissed. The reality of seeing the man was disconcerting.

She chose four more pieces and patiently waited while he finished up with the other customer.

"I see you've found some more," he said. "Would you like a price now?"

She smiled and nodded and they negotiated a price. As she was paying, she casually asked if he had any other merchandise for sale. He looked at her with the same dead stare as his twin and said he had more but wasn't able to take them out of his car just yet.

"I'm really interested in buying anything of this quality and jewelry too, if you have it."

He looked her up and down, running a finger against his

chin stubble and invited her to come back just after closing time, when he planned to leave, in about five hours. He said he would call a friend who could bring other things for her to look at as well when he got a chance, as she was now a "good customer." She hesitated for effect then confirmed that they would return later.

CHAPTER 15

Feeling both shaky and confident at this new turn of events, Veronica and Diane sought refuge at the dairy bar down the street where they both ordered ice cream sundaes. "I feel as though we're in some kind of time warp," said Diane, wiping hot fudge from the corner of her mouth.

"It certainly is surreal seeing a dead ringer for Fiske whom we know is in jail, selling Mattie's clothing at the same flea market. If we hadn't come down here this morning and seen him with our own eyes, I would never have believed it possible."

Suddenly, she had an idea. She reached over to the backseat for her purchases and started to feel along the hem of one of the dresses. "Quick, Diane, give me the scissors in my tote bag." She started to remove the tiny stitches along the bottom of the dress, pressing carefully against the cloth.

"Eureka!" she cried, pulling a string of perfectly matched pearls out of the now-exposed hem. She held them up to the light as Diane leaned over to examine them.

"They're so beautiful and creamy," she said, fingering

them slowly. "I don't know much about pearls, but these seem to glow in the light. Do you think they're real, Ronnie?"

Veronica touched the strand to her teeth to feel if the surface was gritty, the test for determining if pearls are genuine. "They sure are, beautiful in color and uniform in size, and the clasp is gold and set with diamonds. What a find! Mattie's not going to believe this when I tell her."

Their resolve to return to the booth grew stronger now that they had found yet another treasure. Soon Veronica was surprised and delighted yet again, this time by discovering a diamond and platinum bar pin sewn into one of the side seams of another dress. They wondered what had happened to Mattie's original maid, Daisy, and why she had packed away the clothes without ever retrieving the jewelry. Surely Mattie must have missed seeing these wonderful pieces and questioned their whereabouts. Did she really own so much that she considered these as trifles and not worth worrying about?

And the clothing, too, all designed and handmade in Paris by the most famous names in fashion of their day. For Veronica, these garments were timeless pieces that never went out of style and were even more in demand today than when they were when made more than seventy-five years ago. The fabrics were no longer available, and it would be too cost prohibitive to try to duplicate them today. An exception would be the Fortuny pleated velvet that was used to make the Chinese-style jackets. That cloth is still being woven in Italy using the old secret method of folding, known only to the manufacturer. Veronica happened to know that the price of that fabric alone ran to the hundreds of dollars per yard. The pieces she just purchased didn't even have moth or handling damage, a miracle, given their age.

Veronica was also aware that the Chanel dresses alone would realize up to $5,000 each in today's hot auction market for famous designer vintage clothing; perhaps more, given their excellent condition. She guessed that Mattie wore each dress probably only once, certainly no more than twice. Not to mention the treasure trove of precious antique jewelry she recovered from the seams, most custom designed and signed by the famous jewelers of the period who made them . . . Cartier, Belperron, Boucheron, and Van Cleef & Arpels. Yes, they were definitely going back to the flea market later to look at more!

Diane broke into her reverie. "When are you going to call Harry and give him an updated report?"

"I think we should wait until we get all the garments from the twin. I'll ask to go to his house and see what other merchandise he has, and then Harry and Lieutenant Balducci can catch him in the act."

"Not a good idea," said Diane, suddenly alarmed. "What if he shows up with someone else and a gun?"

Veronica considered. "Why would he? He doesn't know who we are and that we recognize him as the twin. We need to ingratiate ourselves as good buyers first, the perfect cover; then we can tell the police to move in." They argued back and forth, and finally, Diane reluctantly gave in.

"Let's go back to my store and rest before we return to the flea market at dusk." Diane agreed but first excused herself to use the restroom.

CHAPTER 16

Justine had formulated a plan based on the information David Daniels had provided. One of his country club golfing buddies owned a big construction company that had just obtained a large contract to build multiple retirement communities on the North Shore. The man was confident and flush and took the opportunity to tell Daniels that he was going to be depositing a large chunk of cash in his safety deposit box at the bank. He winked and said that the money represented his proceeds from a sweetheart deal, and Uncle Sam was not going to be informed of that any time soon.

He suggested that if Daniels himself could take the tote bag of cash, along with his box key and make the deposit himself, it would make life easier for him. He couldn't afford to be seen by anyone depositing this money himself. Of course, he wouldn't forget this favor and would duly reward his buddy, the bank vice president. Daniels smiled as they shook hands, already planning in his head ways to spend the new found money.

Justine realized a golden opportunity when she heard one and Daniels had just provided her with a chance to get her hands on a windfall. She called her brother John and told him to get in touch with Louie and Harold so they could meet to discuss relieving the man of his cash. They agreed to gather at Justine's house at 7:00 that evening when she would have a plan in place.

Daniels had dug his own grave yet again. It seemed he had developed a real weakness for young girls and had recently started to do business with a specialist escort agency in Boston. He couldn't be seen indulging his fantasies in Bromfield, of course, and the sudden flurry of "business appointments" on his calendar was not lost on Justine. She knew his computer pass code and was able to trace the escort agency online. When she confronted her boss with his latest peccadillo, he broke down and told her about the bag of money scheme. This was the break she was looking for.

When John arrived at her house that evening, his dejected look alerted her to a serious problem. It seemed that "Three Fingers" Harry and Louie, "The Blade," had been fingered in the murder of a small-time thief at the Bromfield Flea Market. Talk about bad timing! After it was established that the police couldn't link John with the murder, Justine and her brother had to work alone on this new scheme. They both realized that this was a once-in-a-lifetime opportunity.

Justine now had her boss under her thumb, and if anything went wrong with her plan, she planned to use him as the fall guy. And, if she played her cards right, brother and sister would fall instantly into more cash than they had ever seen.

The realization that she was calling the shots now and formulating the plans spurred Justine on. For years she had been under Earl's thumb, putting up with his snide remarks about him being the brains in the family and her place of value was in the kitchen and the bedroom. He took pleasure in beating down her sense of self-worth at every opportunity and occasionally beating her literally. She had always yearned to align herself with a man who recognized her unique talent for organization and cool thinking under pressure. She constantly saw most of the jewelry the gang stole, that she lusted after, being broken apart or sold to others when she could own and wear them herself, and it really bothered her. The chance to look like a queen in front of her own mirror was an image she just couldn't get out of her mind. Earl never understood or cared about that. He berated her further by telling her how stupid she was and constantly reminded her that she couldn't even wear the stuff in public.

She was glad he was not there to call the shots any longer. John now seemed to be coming around and realizing that she was the true brains in the family, and, if he knew what was good for him, would recognize that only she was able to find a way to elevate him beyond his lifelong "black sheep" status. All he had to do was follow her instructions to the letter and they would both be set for life.

CHAPTER 17

Time seemed to drag by while they waited to return to the flea market. Veronica hung up her latest purchases, and they admired again the superb workmanship and styling that was the best that money could buy at that time they were made. She wished she could keep everything she bought but knew they were evidence in a murder investigation. The jewelry was exquisite too, and even though she was not an expert in diamonds and precious stones, she estimated the pearl necklace alone to be worth more than three thousand dollars, and much more if they were natural and not cultured; the bar pin perhaps another two thousand.

With the capture of both Fiske and Ivy, the police could move ahead with the case against them as thieves, abductors and swindlers. But now, with this new turn of events, the twin and his accomplice would be exposed as well, along with any other proof they could uncover, proving that Mattie wasn't their only victim.

Veronica wanted justice for Mattie and saw herself as an avenging angel for the sweet old lady who had become her friend. The thought that someone would hurt her—and worse—made her blood boil, and because Mattie reminded her so much of her beloved Aunt Gillian, Veronica vowed to see this through and do whatever she could to bring these people to justice. The spunk and resolve she inherited from Gillian were now more evident than ever before.

Diane sat quietly by and realized that nothing she could say would be enough to talk her friend out of not returning to the flea market. She knew Veronica well enough to know that once she had made up her mind, no one would be able to talk her out of anything. As the widow of a thief, Diane knew just what was at stake. She had long ago given up on Carl as a kind and caring husband. His drive to make quick money, no matter what was involved, and his choice of dubious friends had made him a willing pawn in their get-rich schemes. This greedy gang was just the same. She had seen it all before. Diane realized that once the line was drawn, there was no stopping them. Anyone who was unfortunate enough to get in their way was in grave danger and she started to feel anxious and uncomfortable at what might be ahead for them when they returned later to the flea market.

The hours ticked by slowly while they drank more cups of coffee until dusk started to settle in. Veronica wished she had a weapon to take along as an insurance policy. Harry had suggested that as a new business owner she should buy a gun and take shooting lessons, but she resisted, thinking that violence would never be a part of her job. She did have a can of mace, however, and decided to take it along with her . . . just in case—no need to bother mentioning the mace to Diane. Why worry her, she thought, and why tell her I'm feeling a tingle down my spine?

It was time to go. Before Veronica closed the shop lights, she glanced over to the picture of Aunt Gillian who remained her inspiration in all things. She said a silent prayer that her plan would not go badly and instead, concentrated on the voice in her head that said she was doing this for all the right reasons.

The Bromfield Flea Market was now officially closed. There were no cars visible on the property from the highway. Wood barriers blocked the entrance and exit roads. Without the foot traffic, dealers, and food concessions, the market looked like just another empty hay field, which it was. A copse of maple trees to the right of the entrance hid a weathered red barn that was used for storage and now looked slightly sinister in the fading light. The empty parking lot with aisles that were marked with rope and little yellow flags on stakes in the ground flapped silently in the gloom. Occasionally, a car would go by on the main road, but this rural market was a destination only when it was open for business, one day a week, weather permitting.

As Veronica pulled off the main road, she wondered why she had never bothered to ask the twin's name. Diane got out of the car and pushed aside two of the barriers, leaving enough room for them to drive through to the back fields. The tall grass and prickly berry bushes that grew abundantly around the perimeter stood as silent sentries to the sound of her car tires kicking up pebbles.

They spotted the lone van at the very back under the darkening shadows of a ring of trees and recognized the man leaning against the rear bumper, smoking a cigarette, waiting for them. Veronica parked her car nose to nose with the truck. Then they got out and greeted him. All at once another man materialized carrying a large cardboard box.

"This is my friend," said the twin and waved a hand in his direction without giving a name.

"I'm really looking forward to seeing what you have," said Veronica, forcing herself to sound upbeat and jovial. She and Diane walked over to the carton and peered in. It was packed with more clothing, but none appeared to be of the quality that Mattie owned. She frowned and looked up. "These aren't nearly as nice as the pieces I bought this morning. Do you have anything else I can look at?"

The twin nodded at the other man who returned with a new box. The items inside were just as mediocre; modern clothing she had no interest in.

"I'm really disappointed," said Veronica. "I thought you had other similar pieces, nice merchandise of the same age, and vintage items that I would love to buy."

He smiled his rictus smile. "I've got some jewelry here you will like," he said and pointed to the front seat of the truck. Veronica hesitated a moment, thinking she should hold her ground. When she didn't respond, he reached into his pocket and held up a beautiful enameled Art Deco mesh purse. The pattern was like an oriental carpet in blues, reds, and cream, and the fringe swayed with the movement of his hand. She rushed over and held it with reverence. She clicked open the top and realized, even without her loupe, that it was solid gold. The frame had precious jewels embedded in it in a floral pattern and the thumb piece was a sugarloaf cut blue sapphire cabochon stone.

"This is more like it," she said, smiling in spite of herself. "What else do you have?"

He pointed again, wordlessly, to the front seat. Her eyes followed his finger to a large and beautiful box of sterling silver with raised designs of cherubs and flower garlands on the front and decorative little feet on the bottom. As she leaned over and reached for it, she heard a shuffle and a sudden gasp and swiveled around just in time to see the other man with his arm in a choke hold around Diane's neck.

Veronica started to run to her friend, but the twin was too fast for her. He rushed and grabbed her from behind and pushed her against the car, then threw a scarf around her neck.

"You thought I wouldn't recognize you, didn't you, bitch?" he snarled. "My brother Pavlo made his one phone call from jail to me. I know it was you who turned him in and now you're gonna pay."

The scarf pulled tighter around her neck as she kicked back with her right foot against his kneecap. She wasn't wearing sneakers this time but shoes with a heel and, as it hit its mark, he yelped. The scarf loosened a bit but she still couldn't get away. She jammed her elbow into his solar plexus, and he yelped again, this time, moving his body weight to the right. She was able to move in the opposite direction and wriggle out of his grip while trying to shove her hand in her pocket to find the can of mace. Momentarily stunned, he reached out and quickly grabbed hold of her sweater, pulling her back once again.

Veronica knew she was in trouble now. All she could think of was getting away from this fiend who was trying to choke her to death. She could hear Diane gasping for breath, and she knew her window of opportunity to get away was very short. With all her strength, she pulled the one arm that wasn't pinned behind her back up and out and reached up with her long, crimson nails and found his face. She raked her fingers down his cheek, hoping to draw blood, and at the same time, kicking behind with her foot. He yelped in pain but recovered enough to try to pin her other arm back.

She turned and saw Diane struggling hard to free herself from the other man's grip. Then she heard her scream while he pushed her to the ground, the element of surprise working against her.

Suddenly, voices were yelling "Freeze!" and she felt rough hands pulling her away. She looked up to see Harry and Lieutenant Balducci pointing guns at the twin while several uniformed police officers surrounded Diane and pulled her from her assailant.

"Oh, Harry," she coughed, holding her throat. "You're really here!"

"Yes, dearest, I'm really here," and he held her tightly as

she sobbed into his shoulder.

Everything happened very quickly then. Sirens and police cars with flashing lights appeared and the two suspects were pushed into a van under heavy guard. Lieutenant Balducci told her to sit down and rest before he asked some questions. Diane was shaking and clutching her throat too, and Veronica went over and hugged her in a tight embrace. "I'm so sorry I got you into all this," whispered Veronica. "Please tell me you're all right."

Diane recovered enough to smile weakly at her friend and nod her head.

"How did you know we were here?" Veronica asked Balducci.

"I can answer that," whispered Diane, gently rubbing her throat. "I called Harry while we were at the ice cream stand and told him what we were planning to do . . . and he was livid."

"Of all the harebrained ideas you've ever had, Veronica Howard, this has *got* to be the worst," he cried. "Thank God, Diane had the good sense to call me in enough time so the lieutenant could put a plan into place."

"I've got lots of questions for you, Miss Howard, and I know you'll give me lots of answers. Let's all go down to the station, and I'll take your statements while events are still fresh in your minds."

CHAPTER 18

That evening the Bromfield Police Station was a beehive of activity. The two new prisoners were processed through the system, and mug shots were taken, fingerprints recorded, and then they were led to cells. Officer Anderson, Lieutenant Balducci, Harry, Veronica, and Diane all settled down for a long session of questions and statements in a small room at the back of the station. The coffee machine in the corner gurgled and steamed as cup after cup was made and consumed.

Veronica spoke of her realization that morning that Fiske had an identical twin who was continuing to sell Mattie's clothing and jewelry at bargain basement prices at the flea market. When she heard he had more of her belongings, they arranged to meet him after closing in order to purchase more evidence against his brother and to retrieve what rightfully belonged to Mattie.

Diane recounted her friend's dogged determination to bring the thieves to justice at any cost, which included using a can of mace. That brought a laugh from everyone at the table, including Veronica. She also mentioned the beautiful pearl necklace and the diamond and platinum bar pin that she reluctantly handed over as evidence.

"When things started to get ugly and we realized the twin and his buddy were on to us, we knew we were outclassed and outnumbered," said Veronica, rubbing her still sore neck gingerly.

Lieutenant Balducci spoke up while reaching for a licorice stick. "We now know the identical twin, whose name is Vlad Sidlauski, is also wanted by the Chicago P.D. They are here in this country as illegal immigrants. Thanks to Mr. Hunt's FBI connections, we understand they came over the border from Canada about two years ago. Our Canadian neighbors would be very happy for us to extradite them as they were a two-man crime spree up there. They specialize in posing as domestic servants in the homes of the very wealthy and elderly, then get these old folks to sign over their estates to them. Surprisingly enough, they have had a successful track record doing this. The banks have cooperated with us and we know Pavlo has several millions of dollars stashed away."

"No wonder they don't sell the clothing and art objects for a lot of money," observed Veronica. "The big payout is in the will scam. What about the families of the victims? Aren't they even suspicious that something odd is going on?"

Harry answered. "The FBI has been aware of this pair's activities for some time. There was a murder last year in Michigan of a wealthy elderly man in the early stages of Alzheimer's disease. His family was not aware that he had signed over his vast real estate holdings to his 'devoted butler and friend' until after his death. They tried to break the will, and that's when the Sidlauski brothers and their scheme were discovered."

Lieutenant Balducci continued. "By systematically drugging Mrs. Van Brockhurst, who refused to sign her estate over to them, they had hoped to break her spirit and then planned to take her away from Bromfield by boat, kill her, and dispose of her body in the ocean. We caught up with the sleazy maid, Ivy, and the crooked Dr. Slattery just in time, as you already know. Slattery and the captain are currently in custody awaiting trial, with Ivy soon to follow. We have enough of a case against them to put them all away for a very long time."

He shook his head. "You took an awful risk, ladies, by going to a darkened field in the middle of nowhere by yourselves to try to take matters into your own hands."

He pointed the licorice stick at Veronica. "These bozos are career criminals, and I hate to think what would have happened to you both if Mrs. Andrews here hadn't called Mr. Hunt to alert him."

"That can of mace didn't do you much good, did it?" laughed Harry.

"All right, all right," she cringed. "I've been duly chastised."

"If only I could believe that," he quipped, winking at the group around the table.

CHAPTER 19

Justine sat at her kitchen table trying to work out a plan to rob the bank vault. Daniels had reluctantly told her that one of the bank's best customers, the developer of a large condominium project in town, had just returned from a trip to Las Vegas and had experienced good luck at the craps table. And, as added frosting on the cake, his wife hit the jackpot on a dollar progressive slot machine in the hotel lobby as they were waiting for their limousine ride to the airport to fly home. They were feeling flush and the wife wanted some nice jewelry to show the girls at the next country club luncheon. They postponed their flight and told the limousine driver to turn around and take them to the best stores on the Strip. The delighted salesman at Tiffany & Co. mentally totaled up his next commission check and realized it was going to be very substantial thanks to this sale.

Justine, however, was not aware that her brother John, always the black sheep of the family, was acquainted with the Sidlauski twins of Montreal and occasionally acted as a fence for the antique jewelry they stole. John loved to gamble and his weakness for sports betting had recently gotten way out of hand. He knew the brothers had latched on to a lucrative scheme of robbing the rich and elderly by posing as professional butlers on their estates and were able to ingratiate themselves with their employers, most of whom were lonely, isolated, and without family. They had perfected the proper demeanor for the job and their references, which were seldom questioned, were complete works of fiction. The downside was that they had to invest time in their plan to pull it off.

John never participated in these estate scams but lately, he had to get extra money to cover his mounting gambling debts and realized he had to do so quickly. The Sidlauski twins were currently in jail, and thankfully, no one had come knocking at his door to arrest him as an accessory. Still, he needed cash soon, and he couldn't ask his sister for any more loans, especially now that she had taken over Earl's spot as the planner. She claimed to have big ideas but as of right now, he couldn't wait any longer.

Recently he had seen a sign in a store window on Posy Place in downtown Bromfield that announced *"Always Buying Antique & Vintage Items,"* and he hatched a plan based on this. The store, Veronica's Vintage, looked like a nice place, so he decided to call the owner for an appointment to show her some lower-end jewelry he had accumulated to scrap when the price of gold increased.

His appointment was for the following day, and he chose late afternoon to meet, figuring the store would be quiet at that time. He planned to go back and rob the store the next night if the inventory of jewelry she had was sufficient enough to get him some quick cash.

When he walked in and saw Veronica sitting at her desk, he did a double take. What a beauty, he thought. He never did put much stock in that old adage, "Men never make passes at a woman who wears glasses." No, he thought, this one is nice . . . real nice.

Veronica took off her red harlequin spectacles and stood up and walked over to shake his hand.

"Mr. Jones?" she asked, smiling. "How do you do? I'm Veronica Howard."

John wasn't bad looking; in fact, some would say he was handsome. He wore his dark blond hair clipped short, and it suited his features of a strong jaw line, straight nose, and athletic build. He was never at a loss for female company whenever he wanted it, and he knew she was looking him over too.

She invited him to sit across from her desk. He mentally took note of her shapely legs and form and decided that casing this store was going to be an enjoyable experience. He noted there was no wedding ring on her finger and that was always a good sign, not that it ever kept him from pursuing a woman he wanted.

"How may I help you today?" she asked. "You mentioned on the phone you had some gold rings for sale?"

"Yes, I recently noticed your sign in the window and decided to show you some things I have that I want to sell." He took out a small cardboard box from his jacket pocket and placed it on the desk.

She reached for her jeweler's loupe, opened the box, and tipped out the contents on to her desk. There were eight gold rings from the 1950s and 1960s, most with tiny stones and in various sizes. She lined them up then took the largest ring and held it up to the loupe. She looks like she knows what she's doing, he thought, which may or may not be a good thing. It will be interesting to see where this visit goes.

She picked up two or three more, examining them in the same fashion, then put them back on the desk. "May I ask where you acquired this collection, Mr. Jones?"

"Some of them belong to my sister and two or three others I bought from a friend who needed the money."

She nodded and folded her hands on her lap and sighed. "Well, to be honest, my customers tend to prefer either large, vintage '50s and '60s cocktail-style rings with big stones or antique jewelry; gold or platinum Edwardian or Deco pieces, with small diamonds."

Just then the bell tinkled over the door to let her know another customer had arrived. Veronica excused herself and suggested he look at her better jewelry case across the floor to illustrate what she had in stock as examples. He watched her walk away and smiled at the pleasant view of her swaying hips. Keep your eye on the prize, Johnny, he said to himself, as he looked around the shop to check for signs of a safe and surveillance cameras.

He got up and walked over and immediately took notice of some choice pieces in the ring tray. Very nice, he thought.

These will bring me a good night's pay. He also noticed a nice pair of platinum and pave diamond cuff links in the shape of horse heads and a matching tie bar with a horse and crop in pave diamonds. They will bring a good price too, he thought.

She walked back a few minutes later after the customer left. "What do you have in high-grade watches?" he asked. "I'm always interested in buying them."

"Pocket or wrist?" she asked.

"Both," he said, and she reached in and took out two vintage men's wristwatches; a gold Rolex and a gold-filled Omega. He noted she had several very nice Hunter case gold pocket watches as well as accessories of chains and fobs, but he didn't want to appear to be too greedy and didn't ask to see them.

He pretended not to know about the wristwatches and asked her about their history. "I know these are good names," he said haltingly, and she launched into a thorough and informative sales patter on both pieces.

Finally, he said she had given him a lot to think about and admitted her prices were very good. "I sell a lot of men's jewelry to wives and girlfriends for gifts, and several of my best customers are male."

"Well, I'm sorry we can't do business today," she said, putting the watches back and locking the case. As she spoke the words, she couldn't help but think there was something not quite right about this visit. Her intuition questioned Mr. Jones (if that was, indeed, his real name) and his motives, and Harry always told her to trust her intuition. She had a strong feeling he knew more about jewelry than he was letting on.

"If I ever have any other pieces to sell, may I bring them in to show you?" he asked with a big smile. He was enjoying toying with her. *I wonder if I should ask her for a date. No, better not; keep your eye on the prize is the best way to go.*

"Of course," she said. "Thank you for coming in today." She watched him leave wondering if the purpose of his visit was to buy, or sell . . . or neither.

CHAPTER 20

The phone rang, and Veronica was pleased to hear her old friend Amanda's voice.

"I'm calling to ask if you're free for dinner tonight, Ronnie. I have a client conference on the North Shore that will take less than an hour, and I thought I could come to the store, shop, and go out with my best girlfriend."

"That sounds great. I don't have any plans and was going to work late anyway. Come over when you finish your meeting."

The rest of the afternoon went by slowly, and when Mandy arrived, it was like a breath of fresh air. She was always a sophisticated and lovable kook, thought Veronica, and her short, black cape, knee-high boots and huge leather bucket bag, even though it was summer, was toned down from her usual quirky wardrobe to please the client.

They hugged and caught up on the Boston advertising scene gossip as Mandy flipped through the racks picking out several items to try on. She found two pair of shoes, three dresses, and a pair of earrings, and Veronica was delighted that all this was accomplished in about fifteen minutes.

"No one can ever accuse you of not being able to make

up your mind," laughed Veronica.

"Oh, you know me; I get right to it. Besides, I have to make up for lost time, and who knows when I'll be able to come up this way again."

Veronica wrapped all her purchases, and they decided to leave them at the store and Mandy would pick them up when she was ready to drive home. They went to Mezza Luna, a popular local Italian restaurant for drinks and dinner. It was busy for a weekday night and Veronica waved to several people while they were waiting for their table.

"You should run for mayor, Ronnie; you seem to know everyone in town."

"Don't forget I made all the newspapers last year with that stolen art business."

They sat down and ordered a large bottle of Valpolicella to go along with their manicotti starter. They had a lot to catch up on and laughed their way through the rest of the meal of veal scallopini. Veronica found herself wishing for just a moment that she was back in Boston writing advertising copy as part of a team again. But she loved her job as proprietor of her own shop and being responsible for stocking it with all the things she loved to sell. It gave her great satisfaction to be able to sell one-of-a-kind vintage items to customers like Mandy, who truly appreciated the things she purchased.

While they were perusing the dessert menu, she recounted her visit from Mr. Jones. She said she had a funny feeling about him that she couldn't quite put her finger on.

"Harry always says to go with my intuition, and something tells me this guy wasn't one hundred percent."

"What do you mean? Do you think the rings he was trying to sell you were stolen?"

"Well, they were all different sizes, which is rather unusual, and he said they belonged to a family member as well as purchasing some from a friend. It's possible, I guess, but you can't be too careful. At any rate, they were not anything I could resell. He just made me feel a bit uncomfortable; plus, he was ogling me the whole time."

"What's wrong with that?" said Mandy, waving her wineglass. "You are a beautiful woman and he was celebrating that." The waiter came with their ricotta pie order and their attention returned to the food.

Veronica and Mandy were having such a good time and it was quite late when they finished eating. They decided to cap off the evening by having a cordial at the bar and were among the last patrons to leave the restaurant. Veronica slowly and carefully drove back to the store to pick up Mandy's purchases and suggested she make them both some black coffee and rest a bit before they drove back to Boston.

The rest turned into a snooze in the darkened shop, as they both were feeling the after effects of the wine and liquor. Veronica put her head down on her desk and Mandy pulled up a chair and did the same. Always a light sleeper, Veronica's subconscious suddenly recorded a sound from the roof, then a few minutes later, scratching noises from her back door. Mandy heard it too and woke with a start. Veronica put a finger to her lips, and they crept over to the blue velvet couch that she always hoped to sell but didn't and pulled Mandy behind it.

They held their collective breaths as they heard foot-steps advance to the vicinity of the showcase containing the good jewelry. Next, they heard glass break, then the metallic sound of objects being pushed, and a dull clunk. The burglar was out the door in a flash and Veronica ran after the muffled sound of rubber-soled shoes. She dashed to the alley at the back of the store but could see nothing in the darkness. Defeated, she returned to the store, tears of frustration welling in her eyes.

Mandy ran to her and asked if she saw anything. "No, he was too fast for me, and I wish I didn't have so much to drink because maybe my reflexes would be better, and I could have seen his face." She called Harry and he suggested she call the police immediately.

A squad car arrived quickly and two officers looked around the store. They were surprised the women were present at the time of the robbery, and Veronica recounted the circumstances and was able to give them an inventory of all the items taken. She also told them about the visit from a "Mr. Jones" earlier in the day, his odd behavior, and the fact that all the items she showed him were among the ones stolen. She gave them his description and they suggested she come to the station later to go through mug shots. She said she couldn't be sure, of course, if he were the actual burglar, but the circumstances were too much of a coincidence to think otherwise.

They got clearance from the police to drive back to Boston but not before Mandy commented that she couldn't help but observe that a visit with her friend Ronnie was always exciting. "Forgive the black humor, but there's never a dull moment hanging around with you."

CHAPTER 21

Harry was concerned about Veronica's safety. The story she told about the circumstances surrounding the robbery just didn't seem right to him either. He accompanied her to the police station the next morning so she could peruse the mug books, a tedious process that often didn't yield too much success. However, this was not one of those times and Veronica identified John Harmon immediately. Lieutenant Balducci was alerted, and they sat in his office.

"Hmm," he mused, "this guy always seems to fly just under the radar but he's known to us as a small-time thief and accessory."

"Do you think he could possibly have anything to do with the Sidlauski twins?" asked Harry.

"Great minds think the same," said Balducci, and he pressed the intercom button. "Anderson, see what else we have on Harmon, will you? Something tells me he's not lily white in the Sidlauski affair. He could very well be acting as a fence for the jewelry they were stealing."

Meanwhile, John went back home to examine the fruits of his night's work on his kitchen table. The items he lifted from the vintage store would pay the majority of what he currently owed to his bookie. He felt a tiny twinge of regret that he had to rob such a beautiful woman . . . but that didn't last too long. It serves her right being so nice and gullible, he thought, but at least she has good taste. I had better stay away from Posy Place for a while. Maybe I'll keep the Rolex as a souvenir from the job. Justine doesn't have to know about the robbery. She's been acting so high and mighty lately, showing off with her big ideas.

"That's the trouble with women; they always think they're smarter than men," he said out loud with feeling.

Well, he thought, as long as we can cash in regularly through her job at the bank, I can't really complain. Now let me sell this stuff and move on, and he carefully wrapped the goods before going out the door.

CHAPTER 22

J ustine had just learned that David Daniels was having lunch with his flush real estate developer friend. When he returned to his desk carrying a duffle bag, she followed him into his office, closed the door, sat down, and reminded Daniels again that he owed her. The plan was that he would empty the bag of cash, totaling two hundred fifty thousand dollars, into the customer's bank box, the results of a sweetheart deal with a subcontractor. Justine thought quickly and decided to take an immediate cut of twenty-five thousand dollars.

Daniels balked at this saying he was the only one who knew about the deposit and the blame for a shortfall would be directed to him. She again reminded him that sex with an underage girl would end his career quickly, and he had no other choice but to give her what she demanded. He reluctantly counted out the cash and handed the stack of bills to her. Her smile was like the cat that had just devoured a bowl of cream.

To celebrate her newly acquired cash fund, Justine went shopping for jewelry. She planned on having dinner with her girlfriends the following night and wanted to flaunt a new piece or two. She had heard some of her co-workers talking about Veronica's Vintage and decided to walk over and have a look at their inventory on her lunch break.

Justine liked the look of the shop immediately, and when Veronica inquired if she needed help, she asked to see some of the antique jewelry. Veronica always kept a backup supply of pieces in her safe, and she thanked her lucky stars that she still had some inventory to display after the robber cleaned her out of some of her nicest pieces.

The women chatted as they looked at the stock. Justine was particularly drawn to a lovely antique white gold, diamond, and sapphire lavalier and admired how it twinkled around her neck in the standing mirror on the jewelry cabinet. Veronica told her it was from the Edwardian period of 1901 through 1910 and that calibré-cut blue sapphires were often used to enhance old mine-cut diamonds in period jewelry.

"It might be too dressy to wear at the office," observed Justine, turning her neck to the left and right.

"Oh, I don't know. It's the kind of piece that would look good at any hour of the day. No need to save it just for dressy occasions," noted Veronica. "I wear my antique jewelry all the time, and that pendant would look equally well on a black turtleneck sweater as on a velvet tunic, I think."

Justine was warming to the necklace. She pointed to a ruby and diamond band ring set in 14-karat rose gold in the case. "Tell me about that," she said. Veronica took it out of the showcase and placed it on a black velvet pad. Justine put it on her right hand ring finger and admired it.

"Oh, look, it just fits."

"That's always a good sign," smiled Veronica. "And the good thing about a ring is that it can be worn at any time. This is also from the Edwardian era. Good taste in those days consisted of wearing a different piece of jewelry for every occasion. Just like their food and table settings, the Victorians and Edwardians of means were intent on impressing family and friends. The more jewelry you could afford to own, the better to flaunt. Their formal table settings consisted of separate silver utensils for every dish, with cutlery for fish, meat, and fowl, and finger bowls to use between courses. The same was true with their jewelry. And everything had to be the best quality. If you were intent on impressing, you had to outshine everyone else."

"How well informed you are," said Justine. "And I can see this necklace and the ring are not only in good taste, but they are also made very well."

Veronica believed in the soft sell and always thought the quality of the pieces she sold spoke for themselves. Evidently, her customers thought the same way as she sold a lot of jewelry at her shop.

"I really love antique jewelry, and you have a good inventory," said Justine, focusing in on a wide Victorian bangle bracelet set with a lion's head holding an emerald in its teeth. Veronica reached in and placed the bracelet on the velvet pad. "I had more items as recently as two days ago, but I was robbed," she said. Justine looked up quickly while fastening the bracelet on her wrist. "I'm so sorry to hear that," she said. "Did they catch the robbers?"

"No," said Veronica, "but I was here when it happened, and I think I would recognize the man again."

"It was one man, you say?"

"Yes, and he came to the shop earlier the same day to look in this very case."

"How bold," murmured Justine and quickly glanced at her watch. "I have to get back to work at the bank, but I'm going to take the lavalier and the bracelet today. I may be back for the ring, later."

Veronica boxed and wrapped the two pieces and thanked her for her business. It didn't escape her that the customer paid in cash from a large wad of bills stuffed in her pocketbook. As she handed her a Veronica's Vintage business card, she asked her name.

"Justine," called the woman over her shoulder and hurried out the door.

Veronica was delighted with the large sale and had a feeling the woman would be back to buy the ring. She also had a feeling that she had seen her somewhere before as she looked familiar. Veronica had always been good at remembering names and faces, a particularly valuable resource to possess when you work in retail sales. Usually, expensive purchases like this are made with a credit card, but she was always happy to receive cash too.

That night at dinner, the girls greatly admired Justine's new antique lavalier and bracelet. They were unique pieces, and she basked in the glow of the compliments she received. One of her friends, Dottie, a dentist's wife who was always bragging about her newest jewelry acquisitions, looked particularly jealous, which made Justine feel especially happy. She always did have an eye for quality as she so frequently reminded Earl. Now she could buy what she wanted, when she wanted it and even though it didn't quite make up for Earl's shabby treatment of her jewelry fetish over the years, it certainly helped today. But something was nagging at the back of her mind about the robbery at Veronica's Vintage.

She had no reason in the world to suspect her brother John of any involvement, but she couldn't help but think that this certainly sounded like something he would do . . . going to the place first and showing his face before he robbed it. John would have the audacity and ego to do something like that. I sure hope it wasn't him, she thought. He's not going to screw up any of my plans before I'm good and ready to launch them.

The stress of her brother's antics had always gotten to her, and she would have to take her heart medications and wind down. The cost of them seemed to have skyrocketed lately, and every time she went to the pharmacy to renew her prescriptions, the price went up. You practically have to be a thief these days just to be able to afford your pills, she thought ruefully.

CHAPTER 23

One of the downsides of owning a retail business like Veronica's Vintage is that the insurance premiums on store stock against damage or theft is prohibitively expensive and unfortunately, Veronica did not have insurance on any of the items that were stolen. The loss hurt even more because all of the pieces were antiques, one-of-a-kind jewelry almost one hundred years old, and in some cases, older, and all irreplaceable.

Harry was able to soothe her feelings somewhat by recommending she install state-of-the-art security, also very expensive. She compromised with an updated alarm system that would trip a trigger that would register immediately to the security company's 24/7 monitoring system. The hidden safe in the shop was, thankfully, not compromised this time, and Veronica's backup stock of fine jewelry needed to be updated soon with fresh acquisitions to cover the gap in her inventory.

Harry had placed himself in charge of cheering up Veronica after the robbery. He took her to dinner at one of their favorite Boston restaurants that specialized in Greek cuisine. They ordered a mezze platter of assorted delicacies to start with, including dolmades (stuffed grape leaves), Kalamata olives, feta cheese chunks drizzled with olive oil, and roasted red peppers, all washed down with Retsina, that famous Greek wine with the peculiar but pleasant taste of pine resin. The main course of lamb shish kabab, roasted potatoes, and green beans in tomato sauce left them full and happy. They forced themselves to order dessert and shared a piece of rich baklava and Turkish coffee. The satisfying meal was just what she needed to get her mind off the robbery.

Joe Banks, the local beat policeman, suggested Veronica keep the details of the robbery quiet but local gossip had a way of spreading quickly, especially when it was bad news. Veronica recounted the robbery to Joe during their morning coffee break, and she had come to realize that the man who called himself "Mr. Jones" was probably casing her store under the guise of selling her jewelry.

After she identified his photo at the police station, she couldn't get it out of her head that she had seen him somewhere else recently. Joe promised he would let her know if the Bromfield Police came up with any information as to his capture. "Guys like that have a habit of disappearing quickly, but they always make a mistake sooner or later, and then we'll get him," said Joe. Veronica hoped that he was right.

John Harmon was getting antsy. He was disappointed that the jewelry he stole from that nice-looking broad at the vintage store didn't bring him as much as he thought. The cash he got didn't go far enough to pay off what he owed to his bookie. He knew he would have gotten more money if he had thrown in the Rolex watch, but he liked it and realized he wouldn't be able to buy a new one or steal another anytime soon.

Justine had called for another meeting with him tonight at the diner just outside of town. She was getting a little too big for her britches lately, ordering him around like she used to do when they were kids. That bank job of hers was giving her an attitude, but there didn't seem to be anything else on the horizon, and he needed more money fast.

At least his association with the Sidlauski twins always seemed to bring in a steady cash flow, and he missed that. There was always something to fence, and his cut was immediate. He knew he had to lay low in case he ran into that sexy broad again. Maybe he was pushing it a little too much by showing his face the same day he robbed the place. He had done that several times before on other jobs and had always gotten away with it. It had always given him a laugh knowing that he was able to stick it to the amateurs he robbed. No need to feel guilty now.

"You're getting soft, Johnny Boy," he reprimanded himself out loud. "Don't let a skirt get in the way of quick cash and your so-called conscience."

Justine had to formulate another plan. She needed

more money soon because she had spent all that she took from Daniels and the contractor on jewelry and clothes. No need to cut in John, either. I don't see him coming up with any bright ideas, she thought. I do all the work and he just sits there drinking coffee. The beauty of the safe deposit scam is that I can keep going back to the well as long as I make sure the amount is small. And I just love to see David Daniels squirm. No, she had to come up with another angle.

The idea presented itself to her that very afternoon. Dottie, the smug wife of a dentist friend who always flaunted her jewelry at their bimonthly lunch and dinners, came into the bank and asked for her safe deposit box. Justine was walking through the lobby and saw her. She forced herself to say hello with a smile and asked her why she was there. It seemed that Dottie and her husband were going on another cruise soon, and she wanted to take out some of her jewelry to wear, probably to try to impress everyone with her gaudy taste.

Justine had to admit, though, that her ruby ring was exceptional. That pigeon blood red color was top-of-the-line and priced more than diamonds per carat because of its rarity of size and color. Even Earl would have been impressed. She had bought it on one of their trips to Asia several years ago and bragged about it until Justine was ready to scream. Actually, she would give anything to own it herself. So why couldn't she own it? A plan slowly came together in her head.

John showed up at the diner late as usual, subtly sending a message to his sister that he still tried to retain some sort of control in their relationship. He ordered his usual coffee but then decided he wanted something to eat. As he reached to pick up a menu, Justine noticed a new gold watch on his wrist. While he was studying the choices, she realized the watch was a Rolex. How the hell did he get his hands on a vintage gold Rolex? she wondered. He's never had one before that I know of unless this was part of the lot he stole from that vintage shop that I'm not supposed to know about. The waitress came and they placed their orders while she silently fumed at the thought.

"So, what has my sister come up for us this time?" he asked with undisguised sarcasm.

"You know, John, you could be a little more gracious once in a while," she whined. "I don't see you contributing anything to get us a payday."

"You're supposed to be the brains in the family. So what have you got?"

She outlined her plan to have him go to the house of the owners of the ruby ring and rob them. She had formulated a timetable from which she was able to determine when both husband and wife would be absent at the same time. She was particularly insistent that the robbery takes place during one of her ladies' luncheons. The food would taste all the more delicious because she had planned the whole thing. She could look Dottie straight in the eye and know she was the one who had arranged to rob her. Justine insisted, however, that only the ring be stolen.

"After you take the ring, get out of there fast. Don't be tempted to take anything else. This way she will think she just misplaced it and go crazy trying to find it." She laughed out loud at the audacity of her clever plan.

John thought awhile. "So, we fence the ring, and she's none the wiser. Hmm, a good plan, sister mine. That ruby should bring us a nice piece of change, and I know just who will pay well for it. What have you got against this 'friend,' anyway?"

"She's arrogant and pushy and thinks that what she owns is better than what anyone else has. Sounds a little bit like you, John, doesn't she?"

His coffee cup stopped in midair. "What the hell is bothering you, all of a sudden?"

Justine pointed to his wrist. "That's what's bothering me, that gold Rolex. And I know where you got it," she shouted.

Several heads turned in the surrounding booths to stare.

"Keep your voice down," he snarled.

"You robbed that antique store, Veronica's Vintage, didn't you? I was shopping there the day after and heard all about it from the owner. Something told me that it was you, but I refused to believe that you could be so stupid as to show your face and then hit the place the same night.

What's gotten into you, anyhow?"

"Well, if you must know, I needed quick cash, that's all, and it's none of your business if I pull a job on my own. Do I have to report every little thing to you?"

"Don't you realize, John, that if things go belly-up, it reflects back on me as well? And I would never be so careless as to go around wearing something I stole. If there was anything that Earl used to harp about constantly, it was never to wear any jewelry in public that's hot. You should know that; yet, here you are doing just the opposite."

"Who's going to see me wearing this?" he sulked. "Who would put two and two together and figure out it was me who hit that place?"

"Well I did, and if I can do it, so can someone else. If you must keep the watch, just don't wear it around town, okay? Is that so hard to figure out?"

They arranged to meet again the next night to go over their final plans. Justine had now gotten the confirmation from John that he had robbed that antique store, just as she suspected. He was getting sloppy now; he was always bold, but sloppy and out of control was not part of her plan. Unfortunately, she couldn't afford to involve anyone else in her bank schemes and had to depend on her brother to hold up his end.

So far only David Daniels and John were involved, and she intended to keep it that way. Daniels wasn't going to talk, but John was always a loose cannon, and now she knew she had to watch him like a hawk. He probably needs money for gambling again and can't wait until I put my plan into action. The stress of this is going to kill me if I don't watch out. He isn't going to screw this up for me, she vowed . . . again.

CHAPTER 24

Harry had to go out of town for a few days on art-related business. As a well-known private collector and administrator of his family's foundation, he often had to attend business meetings of the many charitable boards on which he sat. Harry also sat on the board of the Bromfield Bank & Trust and attended their semiannual meetings, one of which was planned for today. Afterward, he had arranged to meet Veronica at the store. She decided to do some banking first, and while waiting in line, was surprised to look up and see the woman who had bought the lavalier and bracelet hurrying in to the conference room with a tray of coffee. She asked the teller who she was and was told her name was Justine Palmer and she worked as the assistant to the vice president.

Presently Justine came out, and Veronica took the opportunity to walk over to her desk and say hello. They exchanged pleasantries and Veronica mentioned that her boyfriend was attending the meeting. She thought it odd that Justine became abrupt all of a sudden but dismissed it because the woman seemed to be busy.

Business had been slow at Veronica's Vintage and

Harry's visit was a nice change. She made coffee for them at her shop and asked how the meeting went. He told her he had heard some unfavorable gossip about the vice president, and Veronica mentioned that his assistant had just become a customer.

"What did you hear?" she asked.

"Well, you know how these things get around, but I was told that David Daniels had once been in an inappropriate relationship with an underage girl. It may or may not be true, but something like that can really kill a career."

"Well, he's still working there, so I guess no one took the gossip seriously. You know, Harry, I keep thinking I've seen his assistant somewhere before, and not just as my new customer. You know how good I am at remembering faces."

"Well, sweetheart, can you stand to look at this face at dinner tonight? I have to get back to Boston soon but come to the house at 7:00."

Harry lived on Beacon Hill in a mansion that had been owned by generations of his family since before the turn of the century. He employed a chef who was trained at the Cordon Bleu in Paris. Tonight, Chef prepared a crown roast of pork for the delighted pair and a dessert of an apple and goat cheese tart. They sat in the living room drinking their coffee and listening to the soothing strains of Beethoven's *Pastoral*. Harry asked her a question and didn't get an answer.

"Hello . . . calling Veronica Howard . . . Is anyone home?"

"Now I know where I've seen Justine Palmer's face

before!" she suddenly blurted out.

"Is that so earth-shattering, my darling?" he asked languidly.

"Yes, because it's the same face that cased my store. Either that, or she has a male double somewhere."

Harry put his coffee cup down. "Are you sure about this?"

"Yes, I'm positive. Justine has to be related to the so-called Mr. Jones who tried to sell me some jewelry and whom I'm pretty sure robbed the store."

Lieutenant Balducci was advised of this revelation the next day and was able to confirm that Justine Harmon Palmer had a brother by the name of John who had done jail time for his part as an accessory in a jewelry store robbery. It also came to light that Justine's late husband, Earl, had been killed in an attempted robbery of another jewelry store. The pieces of the puzzle were finally starting to fit together nicely.

Unaware of the case being built against him, John again met with Justine to go over her plan to rob Dottie of her ruby ring. Thanks to her attention to details, she had worked out that the best time for John to break into the house was between noon and 1:30 p.m. the next day. Dottie had mentioned at the last luncheon that there were going to be workmen on the property building a new deck. Justine reasoned they would probably be leaving to take a lunch break during that time. She also knew that both the dentist and his wife would be absent during those hours, one going to his practice and the other attending the lunch with Justine.

All John had to do was rent a generic box truck and drive to the property, looking like another contractor preparing to measure for some additional work. He would bluff his way in with a plausible story, then wait and break into the house. Dottie had once let it slip that she had her own home safe and wouldn't have to rent two safe deposit boxes at the bank. She again cautioned John not to take anything but the ruby ring, and they would meet at the diner at the appointed time later in the evening.

CHAPTER 25

Mrs. Dorothy Simpson loved jewelry . . . loved it so much that her husband, Dr. Seth Simpson, had to caution her on several occasions recently to stop buying because their credit cards were too close to their limits. They had been planning a cruise for several months now and Dottie decided she needed one or two showstoppers to wear while dining at the captain's table. They were frequent travelers on the Sun'N Fun Cruise Line, always booking a premier suite, and the company made sure the Simpsons were given priority treatment. That meant a few new pieces for her fellow travelers to oooh and aaah over; maybe some ruby earrings to match her wonderful ring, her prized possession. And a bracelet would be a nice addition to her collection too. Seth was always carrying on about her spending, but he had made a very comfortable living, especially now that he was in an upscale dental practice building. Who knew there was so much money to be made from crowns and veneers?

Dottie had admired Justine's antique lavalier and bracelet at lunch last week and was surprised that she had the good taste to choose such lovely pieces, quite unlike some of her tackier choices of the past, she thought maliciously. Now, where did she say she bought them? Oh yes, that vintage store, "Veronica's" over on Posy Place. Maybe I'll stop in and see what they have after my manicure appointment tomorrow.

Veronica was just hanging up the phone when the bell tinkled over the door. She looked up to see a well-dressed woman with short blond hair enter and purposefully walk up to her main jewelry case.

"Good morning, I'm Veronica Howard. Are you looking for anything in particular?"

Dottie, always impressed with someone who dressed as well as she did, smiled and introduced herself. She was looking for an unusual piece and would know it when she saw it, she explained; something in diamonds and rubies, perhaps.

Fortunately, Veronica had just put out a lovely girondole pin of ruby and diamonds and a pair of ruby drop earrings just that morning. She took them out of the case and put them on a black velvet pad. Dottie immediately pounced on the pin and held it up to the light.

"I don't often wear pins," she said, "but this is lovely. Tell me about it."

"It's late Edwardian period, about 1908, and is executed in 14K white gold, old mine-cut diamonds, and rubies of good color. I especially like the three drops that fall from the center plaque."

Dottie admired herself in the fancy gilt brass mirror on the counter. "I have a wonderful ruby ring that my husband bought me on one of our cruises years ago, and this would go with it quite well. Tell me, what's the difference between a brooch and a pin?"

"They are one and the same," explained Veronica. "The term is used interchangeably in jewelry. I prefer 'pin' myself."

Dottie continued to look in the mirror. "The stones are small, but their color is exceptionally good; pigeon blood red," said Veronica. "Why don't you try the earrings on? They are not a matched set, of course, but of the same vintage and do go quite well together."

Dottie didn't need any further encouragement and scooped the earrings from the counter, put them on, and again, admired her image in the mirror.

"What do you think?" asked Veronica. "I personally like rubies myself, and these look so well with your short blond haircut."

"Yes, that's what I was thinking too. Not too overpowering and just long enough to be able to wear during the day as well. Do you have anything else in rubies and diamonds you can show me?"

"These are the only quality pieces I have at the moment. I don't know whether you heard, but I had a robbery here at the store about three weeks ago. The thief took a nice ruby and diamond ring, but you say you already have a ring."

"Oh, how awful for you," cried Dottie. "Did they catch him, the thief, I mean?"

"No, unfortunately not, but I was able to identify his photo from the police file. As far as I know, he's still at large."

"Well then, I have to ask you how much for these two pieces."

Dottie was surprised the quoted price was not more, but she had to play hardball, especially when Seth was being so unpleasant about her spending habits of late. She reluctantly took off the pin and earrings and laid them on the counter and sighed.

Just then she noticed a discreet sign on the next counter that stated, "Always Buying." A lightbulb went on in her head. "I have some great, quality jewelry that I no longer wear. Would you consider looking at some of it and if you're interested, perhaps we can apply the purchase price against these two pieces."

"Actually, I do that all the time," said Veronica. "It's important for me to buy quality, high-end pieces for my discerning customers such as yourself. I have a certain level of value and workmanship that I like to maintain, and I'm always interested in looking at fine jewelry as well as vintage designer signed costume jewelry."

"Oh, I have some of that, as well. Well then, please consider these two pieces sold, and I will go home now and look through my safe. I'm sure I can come up with some things that you will want to buy and I'll come back this afternoon. Trading up is a good thing, isn't it?" she laughed.

She was delighted that she could buy these two fabulous pieces of jewelry and weed out some things she was no longer crazy about. Why didn't I think of it before? This woman is so easy to deal with, and with that thought, she tripped out the door with her head in the clouds. I'll have to cancel my lunch with the girls, she thought, easing her Mercedes out of the parking lot. Oh well, I'll call at the last minute. It's more important for me to get those two pieces to wear on the cruise. Seth won't be able to complain that I paid too much because he'll never know I'll be trading in some things he bought me. He never remembers what I have or don't have—only that I'm happy, and I continue to look good.

CHAPTER 26

John had just come back from the truck rental agency with an unmarked cube van. He had given the clerk a counterfeit driver's license for identification from his collection and had taken the precaution to wear a baseball cap that he pulled low over his eyes and a pair of mirrored wraparound sunglasses. He placed a duffle bag containing his tools and a ladder inside to give the impression that he was a contractor looking over an upcoming job. He had a magnetic "ABC Builders" sign that the former gang had made up and occasionally used as a cover and attached it to the side of the truck for authenticity. Justine told him the best time to arrive was between 12:00 noon and 1:30 p.m. He decided to drive through the neighborhood first to see if the deck contractors were still parked in front of the house.

The first time around, they were still working, but about fifteen minutes later, they had left, and he drove the truck around the back of the house to the garage that was not visible to the front and street. John was skilled in safecracking and opening locked doors, as well as being able to soup up cars to go at top speed for quick getaways after a job. He took out the duffle bag and proceeded to make short work of the lock on the family room French doors that opened out to the deck. He entered the house and quickly disarmed the burglar alarm by snipping the wires.

Just as Justine had predicted, the two homeowners were elsewhere. He listened carefully for a minute to determine if there was a dog in the house. Satisfied that there wasn't one, he proceeded to the master bedroom, a good place to start looking for a wall or hidden safe. He was rewarded almost immediately. A bedside table made to look like part of the suite of furniture in the room jumped out at him. He knew from experience and the style and size that it was one of the newer customer-made home safes on the market—expensive, but certainly not a deterrent to someone like him who kept up with these things.

He took off his baseball hat and glasses and sat on the floor, then took out his tool kit from the duffle bag and swung open the door. It would take a little longer to crack this safe open, but he was secure in his knowledge and skills. He applied the pick to the mechanism, intent on getting the job done and exiting the house as quickly as possible.

Dottie looked at her watch again. It was getting to be almost 1:00 p.m. I should have enough time to look over my collection, pick out what I don't wear or want any longer, and get back to Veronica's Vintage before late afternoon, she thought. Stopping to fill up the car with gas, she headed home and pulled up in front of the house so she could return to the store easily without having to put the car back in the garage. She collected the mail from the box next to

GENE REITER
Melrose, MA

Jewelry, Antiques
and Collectibles

Bought and Sold

Phone (781) 662-5678

er key, and entered, placing ev-
Turning around quickly to disarm
 that the light wasn't on. That's
 have forgotten to put it on this
 ıse. I could have sworn I did. She
 her handbag and headed for the

 ıafe and had three trays of jew-
 m. He chuckled and once again
 his clever skills. The ruby ring
 and he held it up to the light. He
 spite of himself. What a find! It
was exquisite both in color and cut. This little baby is going
to bring a nice payday. He put the box down on the carpet
and proceeded to go through the trays. Lots of good stuff
here! Justine's words of caution to take only the ruby ring
still rang in his ears. There's plenty to take here; the woman
won't even miss a couple of pieces. He helped himself to a
sapphire bracelet and two diamond rings and stuffed them
into his jacket pocket.

He hadn't realized he wasn't alone in the room until he
heard a loud, piercing scream. He got up off the floor in a
single fluid movement, took in the scene and ran toward
the door, roughly shoving a startled Dottie out of the way.
It was then that she realized she could identify the robber.
She stumbled, then turned, and ran out after him. She got
to the front door in time to see a white van barreling down
the driveway onto the street.

CHAPTER 27

Things were a little slow at the station house that morning, so Lieutenant Balducci took advantage of the quiet spell to phone Veronica during his coffee break.

"Good morning, Lieutenant. What can I do for you?"

"This is strictly a personal request, Miss Howard, but my wife's birthday is next week and I know she has always preferred nice, older pieces of jewelry. I was wondering if maybe you could suggest something special that's different, something Rose might like. I noticed you had some pretty things on display in your shop when I visited recently."

"Thank you for the compliment, Lieutenant. Does she have a favorite color?"

"Well, let me see. She likes purple and pink and red, of course, because of her name. You know, I'm not very good when it comes to shopping for ladies' things, but I want to surprise her this year because she puts up with me and really deserves a special present."

Veronica could almost see him blushing through the phone. "Let me think about it and see what I have in stock. I'm sure I can come up with a couple of things for you to choose from. Does she like diamonds?"

"Whoa, Miss Howard," he cautioned. "I'm only a lowly servant of the public, you know."

"Don't worry," she laughed. "I have something particular in mind, and the cost would be well within your budget, I'm sure. I'll bring a few things down to the station this afternoon so you can take a look at what I have. If you don't see anything you like, I can make other suggestions as well."

"That's very kind, but I don't want to take you away from the shop."

"My helper, Susan, is working this afternoon. She can watch the store for me. And it would be my pleasure to help you find something nice for Mrs. Balducci."

Veronica hung up the phone, went to the safe, and found several pieces to show him.

The call came into the station not long after Balducci hung up. Mrs. Dorothy Simpson was ushered into his office, dabbing her eyes with a tissue. She had managed to report her face-to-face encounter with the robber to an officer and after filing a report, was invited to view mug shots to help to identify him.

"That's him! That's the man who robbed me; I'm sure of it!" she exclaimed, pointing to a photo of John Harmon. "I only saw him for a minute, but I'd know him anywhere."

Dottie was still at the station when Veronica came in, holding a shopping bag. She was asked to wait and sat on the bench outside the lieutenant's office, also occupied by Dottie. When she saw Dottie in such distress, she asked what was wrong and was given an accurate account of the robbery.

"Could you give the police a description?" asked Veronica.

"They told me his name is John Harmon, and it turns out that I know his sister, Justine Palmer, quite well. In fact, I'm supposed to be having lunch with her this afternoon."

"That's who robbed my store too!" exclaimed Veronica. "And I also know Justine.

⸺⸺◦((◦))◦⸺⸺

The restaurant was busy as usual as the ladies examined their menus. The waiter came over to take their drink orders, and they told him they were waiting for one other person in their party to arrive. Justine was the only one there who was on a lunch hour, but she was nervous for a reason other than the time. John had not called her as she had carefully instructed him to do. She hadn't figured on any problems in her calculations and could only focus on seeing Dottie's face sitting across from her while she was being robbed of her precious ruby ring by Justine's own brother Only Dottie wasn't there.

She reached for a roll to nibble on as she was suddenly feeling a little faint. Her heart was pounding, but she put that down to anxiety. Someone at the table suggested they call Dottie, but the call went to the answering machine.

They agreed it was unlike her to be late and that she was probably on her way or held up in traffic. They decided to go ahead and order because Justine was on her lunch hour.

The small talk throughout the rest of the lunch was driving her crazy. She was getting more and more anxious by the minute and had a nagging suspicion that something had gone wrong. On the other hand, she knew from experience how cocky her brother could be. He was probably sitting in a bar somewhere at this very moment drinking to the success of the job and deliberately not bothering to call her just to have the upper hand and keep her waiting. When the bill came, she paid per portion and excused herself to rush back to the bank. There was no message from John.

In times of stress, Justine experienced a tight feeling in her chest that would eventually go away. She had lived with it her entire life, and she automatically reached for her bottle of pills before calling John. Why wasn't he answering his phone? Her anxiety level was climbing. Take a deep breath, Justine, and just calm down, she told herself. You know that your instructions were clear and John is good at breaking and entering. He will find the safe and take the ruby, and all your troubles will be over.

It was bad enough she couldn't keep the ring. She would give anything to own it—not just because it belonged to that vain and stupid Dottie, but because it would be instantly recognizable as Dottie's signature piece—and stolen, at that. Justine wasn't the type to put jewelry in a safe and know that it was enough that it was there, lying in a box, for her eyes only. No, the fun was in the wearing and the flaunting of the ruby to make other women jealous; to know that she looked like a queen and they didn't, that only she possessed a rare gemstone and what they owned couldn't possibly compare to what she had.

But what if I did keep the ring? she reasoned. I'll be moving away from Bromfield soon anyway, and no one I meet in my new life would ever know it was stolen. Maybe I could plan another robbery and let John keep most of the proceeds so he wouldn't whine about not getting his share of the ring. He knows how much I love jewelry. I have always loved jewelry, and I deserve to own this ring. Her obsession was beginning to have a life of its own.

She swallowed her pills and tried to calm down. Soon her breathing returned to normal and the routine duties of her job took her mind off things until she could call John again.

CHAPTER 28

Harry was scheduled to go to the Bromfield Trust for a short business meeting and decided to stop by the store first to ask Veronica to lunch. Susan told him she had gone to see Lieutenant Balducci at the police station to show him some gift ideas for his wife, so Harry decided to drive there to meet her. He walked in to see Veronica consoling Dorothy Simpson. They had just realized that the same man had robbed them both while the lieutenant was giving instructions to an officer to pick up Justine Palmer and bring her to the station for questioning as to the whereabouts of her brother.

John Harmon was on the run. He drove the rental truck down the Simpson driveway like a bat out of hell and headed toward Boston and the garage he owned to work on his cars. The dilapidated, nondescript neighborhood was the perfect cover he needed, and the room over the garage gave him a safe place to hide out in. It contained a single bed, safecracking tools, a hot plate, and an assortment of handguns hidden under the floorboards.

The silly broad that owned the ring had walked in on him when he was almost ready to leave. He was pretty sure she could recognize him in a lineup. He couldn't let that happen because if they caught him, they would put him away for a long time. He now realized he had left the ring on the floor next to the safe and had only gotten away with the few items he stuffed into his jacket pocket. They would bring him some cash, but nothing compared to what he would have gotten for the ruby. *Justine is probably frantic that I haven't called her,* he thought, *but what am I going to say to her? That I screwed up? That I didn't get the ring? This is just what she needs to hear so she can put me down once again.*

Lieutenant Balducci suggested that Harry and Veronica remain at the station while he questioned Justine Palmer. It was just too much of a coincidence that Dorothy, Justine, and Veronica all knew one another, and two out of three of them were robbed by the same man—the brother of one of them.

When Justine arrived escorted by a uniformed officer, Dorothy ran over to her and screamed, "Why didn't you tell me your brother is a thief? And how would he know I wasn't supposed to be home but instead at a lunch date with you?" Officer Anderson stepped between the two women and told Dorothy to calm down and that her turn to make a statement would come very soon.

Justine was questioned and insisted she had no idea where her brother was or that he was involved in either Veronica's or Dottie's robbery. She said she had heard from him by phone about a week earlier and that he claimed he was not in Bromfield at the time.

However, when she learned that the items stolen from Dottie's home safe did not include a rare and beautiful ruby ring, she clutched at her chest and asked for a glass of water. She signed her statement and was released. She went back to the office and tried to call John once again. This time he answered, and she quietly and calmly asked for an explanation.

John waited for the inevitable tirade from his sister about what a screwup he was and how he never did anything right, but it didn't come. This is not like her, he thought. She sounds tired and quiet, not like the old Justine at all. Maybe she's getting mellow in her old age. They made a date to meet at the usual out-of-town diner later that evening.

Justine hung up from John feeling limp and spent. She accepted that he was never going to change, but worse than that, he deliberately stole other jewelry after she specifically told him not to, and to top it all off, he left the prize piece behind. She could never forgive him for that because she had already made up her mind that the ruby ring was going to be hers to keep.

The office was busy that afternoon, and David Daniels had several appointments scheduled, including a visit with Harry Hunt. When Harry walked up to her desk, Justine greeted him formally and announced him to Daniels over the intercom. Harry played the game and acted as if he had never seen her being questioned at the police station just an hour before. Justine realized that if it ever got out that her brother was about to be arrested, Daniels would go to pieces, and she could very well lose her hold on his silence. After Hunt left, Justine would have a little chat with her boss. She knew she had some decisions to make as she reached again for her heart medication.

CHAPTER 29

John decided he couldn't wait until tonight to meet Justine. His trip to the fence yielded him some ready cash but not enough to disappear for more than a couple of weeks. He would have to see his sister once again for a touch. She owed him that at least because he was the one who took all the risks. Maybe the broad who owned the ruby didn't get a good look at him. After all, it was just seconds before he was out the door and, if she told the cops about the phony license plate and name tag on the side of the van, they could never trace it back to him.

He decided to go to the bank in disguise and hit Justine for money. Then he would cool it for a while and go out of town until things blew over. A nice warm climate would suit him, and he knew a couple of guys he could crash with in Florida until he could get his feet back on the ground. He also knew there were lots of old folks living there; maybe he could use his charm and con his way into some rich old dame's safe deposit box and live a sweet life at the same time. The idea was growing on him by the minute.

Justine was feeling decidedly out of sorts and went to the ladies' room to pat her clammy forehead with cold water. A coworker asked her if she was coming down with the flu, and she smiled weakly and said she was thinking of going home for the rest of the afternoon. She walked back to her office and saw a man with red hair in a window washer's white jumpsuit, holding a bucket with a squeegee inside of it, waiting by her desk. She lurched forward when she recognized John in his disguise and grabbed the corner of her desk for leverage.

"What are you doing here?" she said through gritted teeth. "Are you crazy? Someone could recognize you!"

"No one's going to know it's me in this getup," he said with confidence. "I can't wait until tonight to meet you. Give me some money now so I can get out of town for a while. I need a change of scenery."

"Dottie Simpson fingered you, and so did the woman from the vintage store. The cops know who you are, John."

"What are you talking about? How did they know it was me?"

"I just came from the police station where they were both discussing you, comparing notes, and were able to ID you from mug shots. You've got to get out of here now because they've figured out you pulled both jobs."

"I'm not leaving without my money," he fumed. "I need it to hide out in Florida for a while."

"What about the stuff you took that I distinctly told you to leave behind? Fence that and get out of my sight. You left the ruby ring—my ruby ring, the ring that I've been dreaming about, what I really want more than anything, and screwed up my plan."

"I knew you would bring that up again," he sneered. "You just can't leave it alone, can you? You always have to be the big boss.

"Wait a minute," he said as it dawned on him. "We were going to fence that ring and split the take. You never said anything about keeping it for yourself."

She stood up abruptly. "I deserve to own that ring," she shouted. "I went out on a limb to plan and scheme, only to have you leave without it."

Just then Dorothy Simpson walked in to the bank with Veronica trailing closely behind. They looked over to Justine's desk in time to see a man dressed in a uniform shaking a fist at her. Justine turned, then looked up in horror as she saw Dottie advance on her and holding up her hand with the ruby ring on her finger.

"You miserable little witch," yelled Dottie. "You thought you could steal my ring while I was having lunch with you? Well, it didn't work, did it? Because, here it is, safe and sound, and still on my finger."

Veronica then realized that it was John Harmon standing there in disguise, and she shivered suddenly from the tingle down her spine. At the exact moment of her realization, Harry and David Daniels ran out of the office next door wondering what all the commotion was about.

Veronica yelled, "Harry, it's John Harmon!" and she pointed at him.

Harmon reached into the bucket and pulled out a

handgun, grabbed Veronica, and pointed the gun at her temple.

Everything became slow motion after that.

Harry slid his hand under his jacket and extracted a gun from his shoulder holster and fired point-blank at Harmon, who had just seconds before glanced over to see his sister Justine advancing to Dorothy while clutching at her chest with one hand, and reaching for the ruby ring with the other.

Harmon released his grip on Veronica and slowly slid down to the floor, a neat bullet hole in his forehead. Harry rushed over and grabbed Veronica and they both turned in time to see Justine collapse in a heap on the ground.

Then things happened quickly. Harry called the police and they came with the medical examiner and sealed off the crime scene.

John Harmon was pronounced dead. His sister, Justine, had a fatal heart attack on the spot.

——— ((◉)) ———

Veronica and Harry were asked to see Lieutenant Balducci, and they all sat in his office drinking coffee.

"This is getting to be a habit, don't you think?" he asked sardonically. "As I've said before, murder just seems to follow you two everywhere."

"I just happened to be in the right spot at the right time," said Harry, looking at Veronica and squeezing her hand. "I had to save my girl, and I would do anything for her."

"Congratulations on being a crack shot," said the lieutenant, reaching for a licorice stick.

Officer Anderson came into the office. "The medical examiner has just confirmed that Justine Palmer has suffered from rheumatic heart disease since childhood."

"The stress of her role in the robbery and the part she has played in blackmailing Daniels of the Bromfield Trust proved to be too much for her fragile health," said the lieutenant.

"And speaking of Daniels, we've picked him up for questioning regarding his role in embezzling funds from the bank and from certain customers as well. It looks like he's going to be wearing stripes for a long time.

"In the end, Justine deceived her own brother about stealing the ruby and splitting the take," he went on. "John deceived her by working with the Sidlauski brothers on the side and stealing jewelry without splitting with her.

"By the way, Miss Howard, we were able to recover the Rolex watch he stole from your store. He was wearing it under his window washer's uniform. Just sign for it before you leave the station."

"Thank you, Lieutenant. By the way, have you had a chance to choose a gift for your wife yet?"

"I was looking at some of your things while you both were at the bank. I kind of like this." He held up a diamond and ruby heart pendant set in 14-karat yellow gold and matching chain.

"An excellent choice, Lieutenant. It's an appropriate gift for your lady love because the diamonds are set in a heart form, and the ruby is great for a lady named Rose. I can see you are a true romantic." Then she quoted him a figure.

"Are you sure you can sell this to me at that price and still make a profit? I mean, that's very generous of you."

"I want you to be happy, and Rose will become a 'Veronica girl,' which will make me happy. So, yes, Lieutenant, it's yours for that price."

CHAPTER 30

Harry drove Veronica back to the shop. They recounted their afternoon's adventures to Susan, who could hardly believe it. Veronica gave her the rest of the afternoon off, and they had the place to themselves. She walked over to the picture of Aunt Gillian and stared at it for a while. Harry stood beside her and asked if she was communing with the spirit of her favorite aunt.

"Yes, and I'm thanking my lucky stars I had her in my life and that she wasn't a victim like poor Mattie. They remind me so much of each other, Harry; two ladies who were ahead of their time and lived life to the hilt."

Almost on cue, a vintage silver Rolls-Royce pulled up to the front of Veronica's Vintage. The chauffeur opened the rear door, and a uniformed nurse and a stately elderly lady emerged. The bell tinkled over the front door and Harry and Veronica rushed over to escort Mattie into the shop.

"Hello, dear," she said. "I thought it was time for me to pay a visit to your delightful store."

They sat her down on the blue velvet sofa that never sold and brought her a cup of tea.

"What a charming place you have, Veronica. Why it

looks like an extension of my very own closet. I would be very much at home here, I'm sure."

She explained she had a new nurse, maid, and butler, all professionally vetted by an agency, and her health was back to where it was before the Sidlauski twins entered her life. She had also just engaged the services of an older companion who would keep an eye on her and who was going to start her job next week.

"Please thank your dear mother, Ann, for her help in all this, Harry. I couldn't have done it without her."

"Mother has always been very organized and knows the right agencies to call. She was more than happy to help, Mattie. You can call on her, and us, anytime at all."

"Well, that's what brings me here today, my dears. I wanted to thank you again in person for what you did for me." The front doorbell tinkled, and the chauffeur came in bearing a large dress box and laid it on the counter.

"What's this, Mattie?" asked Veronica.

"Go ahead, dear, open it."

Veronica rushed over and with a squeal of delight, took out several of Mattie's beautiful vintage designer dresses from the tissue paper.

"They are yours to do with whatever you like."

"Oh, I can't accept them, Mattie; they're too precious."

"You must take them, and I want you to know that I am leaving you my entire collection of vintage clothing in my will." She put up her hands in a mock negative gesture while Veronica protested. "I can't think of a better person to own and appreciate them after I'm gone."

"And for you, Harry, a small token of my appreciation." She handed him a red leather box from Cartier. Inside was a beautiful set of platinum, diamond, and mother-of-pearl cuff links and studs from the Art Deco era. "Horace would want you to have them too."

"I shall wear and always treasure them, Mattie. Thank you so much."

They spent a very pleasant hour together; then it was time for her to go. The nurse helped her up and they walked over to the picture of Aunt Gillian. Mattie spent a minute looking at it, then turned to Veronica. "Yes, I can see the resemblance now. I want you to think of me as your aunt Gillian's older sister and remember me fondly."

As they hugged, Mattie winked and slipped a little black box to Harry behind Veronica's back.

When the car drove away, Veronica locked the front door and turned off the lights. She walked back to the counter and looked at the beautiful clothing again, then started to cry.

"What's the matter, dearest?"

"I'm so happy, Harry."

"I'll never understand why women cry when they're happy. I've always wondered about that."

"I have no answer to your question, I'm afraid."

He handed her the black box. "Here's another gift from Matilda Van Brockhurst, your new aunt."

Veronica opened the ring box and cried some more.

Inside was Mattie's 3-carat Art Deco platinum and diamond ring that she had discovered sewn into the hem of the silk velvet Chinese coat so many months ago and fell in love with on the spot.

"Oh, Harry. I can't accept this; it's too precious."

"She wants you to have it, Veronica, because she loves you. You couldn't possibly give it back because it would hurt her deeply."

"But it's worth a fortune."

"Well, that's where Mattie and I think alike. We both feel that you're worth a fortune."

She took the ring out of the box and put it on her finger. It twinkled in the light of her desk lamp and sent a kaleidoscope of color back to her eyes, mesmerizing, as only a fine jewel can do.

"I will treasure this always, just as I treasure her friendship."

She turned off her desk lamp, and they walked out the back door together.

⸺◦((◐))◦⸺

Many thanks to Michael and Sharon Nichols for their technical expertise, help and encouragement. Also a special thank you to my brother, Father Kenneth Gandolfo, for his continued acceptance of my flaws and impatient nature. To all the friends who encouraged me in this endeavor, especially Judith Kozlowski, who has always been supportive as only a good friend can be, my heartfelt thanks.

CPSIA information can be obtained
at www.ICGtesting.com
Printed in the USA
FFHW020730240919
55134354-60844FF

9 781977 211729